The Good Land

by
Kristen Adam

Yattira Publishing

The Good Land
ISBN: 978-1-7326580-1-1
Copyright © 2020 by Kristen Adam

Cover Design by Elizabeth Carlson

Edited by Yattira Editing Services
Published by Yattira Publishing
contact@yattira.com
www.yattira.com

For my beautiful daughters:

You girls have passionately pursued the powerful life-force of love, finding truth and boldness in who God created you to be. Witnessing your journey of self-discovery and transformation has truly been an inspiration! I love you, always.

Chapter 1

Annmarie was dismal and dismayed, as usual, but especially so on this January 18th. She was laying on her lavender and white checkered comforter. Unfortunately, it wasn't doing such a great job of comforting. She wore her winter beanie, socks and slippers to keep herself from freezing in the drafty apartment.

She was on her tablet (compliments of school) and looking for a YouTuber who would make her laugh. Anything to dull the pain of what had happened to her exactly twelve years ago.

"Annmarie! Come out here, and do the dishes, NOW!" Aunt Bonnie yelled from the kitchen. Annmarie let out a sad sigh and dragged herself out from under the warm covers to comply.

Even before she made it into the kitchen, the ranting began, "Listen, Annmarie. I'm tired after a full day of work at the hospital. I don't want to come home to a big pile of

1

dirty dishes. I'm letting you live here, so the least you can do is help out. Who do you think you are? I expect you to do more than hang out in your room all day…" As Aunt Bonnie fumed, removing her white nursing shoes and massaging her feet, Annmarie tuned her out in an attempt to cope.

Bonnie was a single mom of a twelve-year-old boy. Paul was at basketball practice and somehow always got out of doing any chores because he was busy playing sports. Honestly, Annmarie identified quite well with Cinderella.

"Sorry, Aunt Bonnie," Annmarie interrupted.

In response, Aunt Bonnie rolled her eyes in disgust.

Annmarie just turned away and went to the sink and started the water. As the water streamed out of the faucet onto the dirty dishes, so the tears trickled from her eyes. This day never got easier to face.

This isn't what my life was supposed to look like! Annmarie thought to herself.

January 18, twelve years ago, was a normal day. Annmarie's parents, Janet and Jacob Williams, had strapped her tiny body into her car seat. They were on their way to their favorite family restaurant for dinner. While driving east on I-94, a drunk driver fell asleep, spun out and hit their car. Both her parents were killed on impact, while Annmarie escaped with little more than a few scratches. She had been their only child.

Orphaned at just three-years-old, most of the funeral and events surrounding the accident were a blur, but she remembered random snapshots of adults talking and looking at her sadly. The local newspaper printed a front-page headline about the tragedy, so it seemed that everyone in the community knew all about it.

Annmarie's parents had loved her wildly. There were all kinds of pictures of her as a baby. There were pictures at the park, at the pool, at the library. Annmarie loved looking at them. She kept the zip drive of the family pictures in her nightstand and would plug in the pictures often because she didn't want to forget. Annmarie had a copy of a photo Christmas card the family had sent out just weeks before the accident. The card was of Annmarie being kissed by her parents as they held her in front of the Christmas tree.

She was told her parents loved to cook and play tennis together. They had an appreciation for theater and music, but they also loved going to the movies. After meeting on a blind date, they ultimately fell in love. She was told they had plans to buy a houseboat one day and sail around the world. They were strong Christians, but Annmarie wasn't so sure about faith.

This blow to the family had left gaping wounds, anger, and humongous doubts. Even so, Annmarie wanted to believe there was a God because she couldn't understand or process why this had happened. It was like she had been plunged into a black hole.

Janet and Jacob were excited about starting a family. Janet enjoyed building a blossoming photography business out of their home. Jacob had been an accountant at a local firm. Everything was picture perfect, and Annmarie was the joy of their life.

Unfortunately, Janet and Jacob had never prepared a will or purchased life insurance. These were things they would have gotten to in time—but it was too late.

Bonnie was Janet's baby sister, best friend, and only sibling. Bonnie leaned heavily on Janet and had even invited her to be her birthing coach. The two were inseparable and texted each other constantly.

Their parents, Emily and Eli Johnson, had always been very busy people and hard workers. They both worked full-time, and usually overtime, their whole lives. Emily always made sure they had various babysitters when they were really young, but as they got older, Janet and Bonnie became latch-key kids. The sisters were used to being alone, and Janet was Bonnie's mother hen.

When it came time to discuss who should take custody of Annmarie after the accident, Grandma Em and Grandpa Eli heavily insisted that Bonnie take her. After all, she was young and was having a child anyway who would need a playmate. She would do better with kids than they would. They promised to send Bonnie extra finances to help with expenses.

Jacob's father was a widower. He suffered from depression as a result of his wife's death, and Jacob's passing plunged him into deeper despair. He escaped his pain by drinking alcohol. Clearly, he was unfit to care for his granddaughter. He also agreed that Bonnie would be the best fit for taking Annmarie. Bonnie felt she had no choice but to take her niece in. It was that or put her into foster care and she couldn't face doing that to Janet.

Bonnie knew if the tables were turned, Janet would have lovingly volunteered to help, so she took Annmarie into her tiny 2-bedroom apartment. She was pregnant and alone, since the father wasn't in the picture. She had lost her closest friend and sister and now felt overwhelmed by having to care for a three-year old and brand-new baby—all by herself.

Occupied with their own lives, Bonnie's parents never followed through with their offer of assistance. In the beginning, she gave them the benefit of the doubt, knowing they were busy, but over time her resentment grew. Her heart became saturated with not only a tsunami of grief, but intense bitterness as well. Cutting herself off from anyone who might become close to her, with the exception of her own son, Bonnie took out her pain on the one who needed her love the most: little Annmarie.

Chapter 2

Annmarie was in 10th grade at Wauwatosa West High School. She loathed going to school and refused to get involved in any activities. She went to school only because she had to. She was counting down the days until she could graduate, get a job and leave Tosa for good.

Annmarie's grand plan of life after graduation was moving far away and buying a dog. She really loved dogs, but her current reality was, "No pets allowed." A family down the hall had once tried to sneak in a kitten. The apartment managers were so strict, when the neighbors got caught, they were evicted!

Throughout Annmarie's school career she had been very quiet and kept to herself. In fact, she was so quiet that her aunt was called to speak with the school's guidance counselor on multiple occasions. The teachers had a hard time working with Annmarie because she wouldn't participate. Her thick turtle shell insulated her and made her feel safe, so she had no interest in coming out! Eventually, even her teachers gave up trying to encourage any change.

Although Annmarie thought she was too plump, she was actually quite slender. Yet, she hid behind big, oversized clothes and an unkempt appearance. She avoided makeup and wore her light brown hair long, usually hiding most of her face behind it like a curtain. She was deathly afraid of attention, and would rarely meet anyone's eyes, so no one noticed that they were a beautiful soft brown.

Like a chameleon, she had learned to blend into the background. She didn't know how to make friends and was a mystery her peers didn't even want to try to figure out. The kids, and even some teachers, treated her like she was defective because she wouldn't talk. Their cruel words stung and caused her to retreat further into her shell.

Yet, rather than feeling unfairly judged, Annmarie simply reasoned they must be right. The judgmental and harsh words had seeded into her heart, so she thought, *I must be defective.* Even her own aunt treated her like something was wrong with her, and her grandparents didn't have time for her, either.

Second semester had just begun. Annmarie had started a new photography class as an elective. So far, surprisingly, she really liked it. She was learning how to process film and was given an old 35mm camera that the school loaned out, although it seemed like ancient technology to her. She had an assignment due in the next week to take some pictures and process them in black and white.

She hoped it would snow again because she thought about capturing the bare trees blanketed with sparkling snowflakes. That would be cool for contrast. She thought about the contrast between herself and every other "normal kid" and sighed. In Annmarie's eyes, there couldn't be a greater contrast than that one. She remembered her mother had started her own photography business before the accident. Annmarie had a glimmer of hope and thought, *What if this skill runs in the family, and I could be a photographer like Mom?* However, since she felt like she was a failure at everything else, she quickly shut herself down with, *Who am I fooling? Nobody would want my stupid perspective anyways.*

Just as she was finishing up the dishes Bonnie had asked her to wash, Paul burst into the kitchen.

"I *dominated* today in our scrimmage! Coach Carter told me that he was going to move me up to the A team! He said I have potential!" Paul did a little happy dance in front of Annmarie. Since Paul was currently on the basketball "B" team, he considered this a huge victory.

She smirked and gave him a half-hearted nod. Even though she was happy for her cousin, she secretly wished that just once something special like that would happen for her. She fought feelings of wanting to be noticed, but the safety of going *un*noticed was much more tolerable.

"That is so wonderful Paul! I'm so proud of you! All your hard work paid off. You're awesome, bud!" Bonnie squealed with delight. "Just keep it up, Michael Jordan, and one day you'll be a rich and famous man who can buy his mama a mansion! For now, though, get to your homework and throw those putrid socks in the laundry basket. Where's my room deodorizer? Whew!"

Annmarie chuckled. It was no joke! His socks actually smelled like rotting food. Absolutely nauseating.

Even so, Annmarie was glad that Paul was around. He was always a good distraction. Bonnie and Annmarie butted heads, but when Paul was around it was somehow easier.

Still, making a real connection with him was blocked by her resentment. Paul belonged. He was Bonnie's *real* kid. Paul did well in school and in sports and was liked by most everyone. In Annmarie's eyes, Paul had it all together. So, Annmarie continued to wear her misery like a cloak because she knew she wasn't really wanted.

"Annmarie, I have a splitting headache. Pauly has to get to his homework. Put that load of laundry in the machine before you go to bed," Aunt Bonnie ordered as she closed her eyes and popped three ibuprofen tablets.

"Goodnight." Aunt Bonnie rubbed her temples as she sighed, walked into her bedroom, and closed the door.

Paul attempted a three-point shot with his socks into the laundry bin. He then whipped in his stinky practice clothes as well and danced into the bathroom, cheering for himself all the way. "Thanks, A!" he shot over his shoulder as he left in as much of a whirlwind as when he had come.

And then she was alone in the living room. Alone was good and quiet. She flopped down on the couch, took a deep breath, and started beating herself up again as she separated whites from colors. Fresh hot tears streamed down her cheeks as she directed her attention to that destructive voice of self-pity.

Her internal monologue was cruel: *I'm a failure. Unwanted. I'm ugly, and stupid, and no one cares about me. I wish my parents could hug me right now.* Tears came stronger now and she felt unable to control her sobs.

Just then she glanced at her Aunt Bonnie's health magazine on the coffee table. There was a beautiful model on the cover offering joy and happiness to women who followed a specific diet and exercise plan. It didn't even occur to Annmarie that the model was airbrushed, and it was truly not a realistic image.

Maybe that's what I need to do. Maybe if I look like her, I could fit in? The image of a boy from the fourth grade came flooding to her memory. He had looked right into Annmarie's face and called her "fatso" while other kids laughed. It was something she had never forgotten. That comment stung her worse than a thousand hornet stings at once. She winced every time it came back to mind.

That's it! As she slammed down the towel she was sorting, Annmarie made up her mind. *I am going to lose weight!* She couldn't control most things in her life, but her eating was something she *could* control. She wiped her tears away with her sleeve and found that her new idea brought her a bit of relief from the ache inside.

Annmarie got up, quickly threw the load of whites in the washing machine and flopped down on the couch to wait for it to be done. She turned on the television and started watching an old rerun of *The Love Boat*. Before she knew it, she had fallen into a deep sleep.

Walking in a densely wooded park, Annmarie saw a brilliant red cardinal perched proudly on the branch of a tree. She was mesmerized by its beauty and tiptoed toward it to see how close she could get—maybe even close enough to touch it. She got within a few feet before it flew off.

Annmarie knew she had to follow the bird. She noticed she was barefoot on snow-covered ground yet didn't feel cold. She climbed a hill in pursuit of the glorious bird. Once at the top of the hill, she turned around and saw a hole cut into a huge rock, like the entrance to a cave. The cardinal landed right on top of the cave entrance and looked at her. She moved closer to the cardinal and it didn't even flinch. It actually started to glow, and she sensed it was extending her a warm, friendly invitation.

Suddenly, Annmarie woke up with a startled feeling. She rarely ever remembered her dreams, and when she did, they were usually scary. But this dream was different. The cardinal had been stunning—like a flying gemstone! She was in awe and felt curiosity welling up inside her. It had felt so real!

Glancing at the clock in the kitchen, she panicked when she saw that it was 2:22AM.

"EEK!!" She ran through the hallway to the washing machine, pulled out the wet clothes and threw them into the dryer, hoping she wouldn't wake anyone. She noticed a print on the wall that had been there forever. However, it was as if she was really seeing it for the first time. The print was a winter landscape with a cardinal perched on a tree branch. She rubbed her eyes and looked again.

"Wow!" Annmarie muttered with a smirk. "That is crazy." She stood and smiled in contemplation as she gazed into the print for a few minutes. She wondered what it could mean—if it meant anything at all. Most likely she had seen the picture many times before, and her subconscious had chosen to bring it back to her in a dream. Still, she shrugged and peered more closely at the little bird. She touched the cardinal with her pointer finger and whispered, "Gotcha!"

Chapter 3

It was a dreary, freezing Monday morning. Annmarie popped one eye open to see what the world looked like outside her window. All she saw was frost covering the inside and outside of the window with very little light shining through the panes. Annmarie desperately desired to throw her purple and white checked sea of warmth back over her head. She thought about faking being sick but knew it wouldn't make a difference. She could hear Aunt Bonnie's sarcastic laugh, now, "No excuses! I don't get time off, and neither do you!" Annmarie had gone to school many times when she really should have stayed home.

Aunt Bonnie counted on Annmarie walking Paul to school. Even though he was twelve, and fully capable of walking himself, extremely protective Bonnie expected Annmarie to look after him.

The school was within walking distance of their apartment; it was only a ten-minute journey. The high school and the middle school were nestled right next to each other, so they walked to the middle school first and then Annmarie would continue to the high school.

At least Annmarie was kind of looking forward to going to her photography class. The instructor was really artsy and eclectic—she was different than the other teachers. She seemed to understand Annmarie and didn't harass her or call her out in front of the class.

Finally, Annmarie got up and grabbed herself a piece of toast, skipping the butter and jelly. Fewer calories. She made a lunch for Paul, as she was also expected to do, but only grabbed an apple for herself. Annmarie bundled up with a winter hat and mittens. She suggested Paul do the same because it was freezing outside, but Paul shrugged his shoulders and left without the accessories because he was just too cool. His foolishness left her dumbfounded.

As they were walking, Paul yelled out to some friends he saw up ahead and ran to meet them. She noticed all the boys had bare heads and hands. Annmarie rolled her eyes and shook her head in judgement. *How lame*, she thought to herself. *Is it worth frostbite?*

She started reminiscing again about her dream as she looked at the snow on the ground. She contemplated taking her boots off to see if she could walk in the snow barefoot like she had in the dream but merely laughed at herself. She was thinking just as idiotically as those boys!

Suddenly, Annmarie was startled by a tap on her shoulder. She spun around to see a tall, lanky girl. Her sun-kissed blonde hair was pulled up into a messy bun, and strands of escaped hair framed a face wearing not only glasses, but a bubbly smile as well. Honestly, Annmarie thought she looked like she would be more comfortable on a beach than here in Wisconsin.

"Hey, aren't you in my photography class?" the girl asked.

"Who—me?" Annmarie quickly looked away and focused intensely at the snow under their feet.

"Yes! Yes, it is you! I know it's you. You sit in the way back. I noticed you there."

"Um. Yeah. I'm in a photography class."

"Cool. Do you know what you are going to do for your black and white photo assignment?" the girl asked as she started to walk with Annmarie.

"Maybe. I'm not sure." Annmarie answered uncomfortably.

Who is this girl who suddenly came out of the woodwork? Annmarie thought. *I've never noticed her before at school. Why is she talking to me? What does she want? Did someone put her up to this?* Annmarie glanced quickly through her hair to see if anyone was watching.

Unfazed, the girl continued to ramble, "I'm new to Wisconsin. I came from California. We moved because my dad got a new job. I don't really know anyone, but it seems like a nice area. My name is Philomena. I know it's a crazy name, but my friends call me Philly. It's way easier. My parents named me after my great-grandmother. I've thought about changing my name to something more normal but it's okay. I guess you can change your name when you turn eighteen, but you have to pay for it!"

Philly shrugged her shoulders and laughed. "You seem really nice. What's your story?"

Feeling overwhelmed by this unexpected friendly contact, Annmarie felt frozen and just kept looking to the ground as they walked. To say that she lacked social skills was a huge understatement. So, Annmarie simply shrugged her shoulders. Apparently not at all bothered by Annmarie's awkwardness, Philly continued walking and talking, sharing all about herself.

"I'm a sophomore and I don't have any siblings. Do you? I saw you were walking with that boy over there. Is he your brother? I always wanted a brother or a sister, you know? My parents bought a house just down the street from here. It's pretty cool. It has a swimming pool in the back. I wanted to ice skate on it because it's so cold, but my mom said they drained the water out of it. I have a dog named Chewy. He's really cute."

Annmarie's ears perked up when Philly mentioned her dog. She looked up, as this topic had struck a chord.

"Aha! Do you like dogs? Maybe you could come over sometime and meet Chewy. Chewy is short for Chewbacca."

Annmarie certainly was intrigued but still felt confused and uncomfortable.

"This has been a crazy adventure moving here. We never had snow where I lived. This weather here is so different!" They reached the school and Philly waved goodbye.

"See you later, um…What's your name?" But before Annmarie could drum up the courage to answer, Philly shouted "Okay! Bye!" and rushed off to her first class.

All day Annmarie couldn't concentrate in class as she kept thinking about her encounter with Philly. She wondered why Philly even noticed her sitting in the back of their photography class and what would have provoked her to start a conversation, let alone invite her to meet her dog.

Well, Philly is new. She'll learn soon enough that I'm not a friend worth pursuing.

Annmarie's heart raced as she walked down the hallway to her photography class, which was the last of the day. She sat in her usual seat in the back of the room, thinking Philly surely would have forgotten all about that morning.

However, when she arrived, Philly made a beeline to Annmarie's desk. "Hey, you! I didn't catch your name earlier." It seemed like Philly genuinely wanted to know.

"Annmarie."

Philly smiled and shook Annmarie's hand. As the new girl, she was a strange bird to the other kids. Even more so now, as anyone approaching the odd duck in the back was an unusual occurrence. Annmarie felt paralyzed. As their classmates stared at them and whispered behind their hands to one another, Annmarie felt even more like a bug under a microscope.

The teacher, Mrs. Smith, entered the room and ordered the kids to take their seats, and Philly plopped her stuff right down next to Annmarie like it was the most natural thing in the world. Annmarie sensed other kids' disapproval, but Philly obviously didn't care. Mrs. Smith began a lecture on the history of black and white film.

Annmarie snuck a quick glance through her hair at the whirlwind sitting next to her. She was confused and skeptical about Philly's interest in pursuing her as a friend. It just wasn't normal! Then again, Philly was certainly unlike any of the kids Annmarie had ever known.

Back in middle school, Janice Anderson had tried to be her friend. After an initial hesitancy, Annmarie was excited and open to it because Janice had seemed really sincere in wanting to connect. At first, she was nice to Annmarie, but she found out later that Janice had spread rumors and shared her secrets with other kids. Janice had then turned on Annmarie like a roaring lion seeking out her prey. From that time on, Janice had mercilessly bullied Annmarie.

The betrayal had wounded and scarred Annmarie, so she had decided she would not open up to anyone else ever again. Down deep in her heart, she longed to be vulnerable in true friendship, but she was tragically terrified of being hurt and rejected again. Losing her parents had been hard enough—navigating the minefield that friendship could be was just too much for her to handle.

After class ended, Annmarie quickly got up to leave, trying to avoid any further interaction with Philly. Her plan was to walk home and just escape into her bed. Philly followed on Annmarie's heels.

"It is quite amazing that photography has been around almost 200 years, don't you think? Hey, I'm staying after school to check out this yearbook club. Do you want to stay? I was thinking of getting involved. I enjoyed being on the yearbook staff in California, too. I figure it would help me get to know people here quicker, and it might be fun if we checked it out together. What do you say?"

Annmarie scoffed at the suggestion. *Is this girl serious?* That was the last thing she wanted to do.

"Um…No, thanks."

Philly was apparently unaffected by Annmarie's rebuff. "Okay, no problem," she said with a smile and wave. "I'll catch you tomorrow morning, then!"

What is up with that girl? Annmarie wondered. *She is seriously crazy.*

Annmarie trudged home. She was tired and still not feeling the greatest. Her mind was set on slipping into her cocoon of covers. Her palace of peace. As she traveled, she carefully scanned down the streets to spot homes with swimming pools in the backyard. She wondered if she'd ever get a chance to take a dip with Philly and her dog.

Then, shaking herself back into reality, she chastised herself. *Who am I kidding?*

Chapter 4

Aunt Bonnie was a nursing assistant and worked at Elmbrook Hospital, so she had some crazy hours. Usually during the week, she worked second shift, so she and Annmarie were like two ships passing in the night. On the weekends, Aunt Bonnie sometimes worked, but the hours varied from week to week.

On this particular afternoon, it was more like two ships crashing into one another, rather than peacefully passing by. Bonnie bombarded Annmarie as soon as she entered the apartment.

"Annmarie, you forgot to fold these clothes last night! Finish it! I put some frozen pizzas in the freezer. When Pauly gets home from practice, just pop these in, otherwise there is leftover chili from a few days ago. Oh, and please make sure Pauly gets his homework done, and *insist* he gets in the shower."

Annmarie mutely nodded her head, grabbed the clothes and sat down on the couch to fold them.

As Aunt Bonnie zipped her coat, she shared that the hospital had called her to come in a bit early, and off she flew out the door.

When Annmarie was younger, she used to feel abandoned and frightened when she was alone in the apartment. There were lots of different noises and smells that came from all around. However, now she quite liked being alone.

She was really grateful for Ms. Opal, a little old woman who lived two doors down. She may have been an elderly lady, but she was loud, round and funny and didn't take any garbage from anyone.

One night, when Annmarie was about nine years old, she had been home alone with Paul, who was only six. There was a loud party in the apartment directly above theirs. They could hear swearing, fighting, with the accompaniment of loud, inappropriate music. Paul had been terrified and was crying inconsolably.

Annmarie hadn't known what to do, so she took Paul by the hand and led him to Ms. Opal's apartment. At Annmarie's timid knock, Ms. Opal came to the door in her dressing gown and plastic nightcap.

When she opened her door to see the children trembling with fear, and heard the violent ruckus, she told them to go into her apartment and said, "Oh, no, sir! We are *not* having these shenanigans here!"

Annmarie had cracked open the door to see the old woman marching boldly right up those stairs! To this day, Annmarie wondered what exactly had happened that night, because shortly after Ms. Opal returned, the police had come and dragged everyone out of that apartment!

So, Annmarie felt safe with Ms. Opal around. Not only that, she also had a flair for baking and always invited the kids over to enjoy her cookies, brownies, cakes or pies. Annmarie knew she was always welcome at Ms. Opal's.

Annmarie finished folding the clothes. She made a pile

for Paul, another for Aunt Bonnie and put them aside. Then she took her own clothes and just stuffed them in her drawers. She didn't care if they were folded or not.

Finally, she crashed on her bed and lost herself on her cell phone, searching black and white photography. She really wanted to take some time and get inspired about what to photograph for her big assignment. She looked at different images online. She saw a super cool lion. *Too bad there aren't any lions strolling around my neighborhood that I can take pictures of.*

She spotted a picture of a woman with some round glasses on that glinted with the reflection of a house. She saw hot air balloons, landscapes, water and close-ups of faces and eyes. She even saw pictures of flowers and fruit. It was really fun to just imagine what it must've been like to take some of those pictures. *Although*, Annmarie thought, *no way would I ever go in a hot air balloon. No way!*

Then she saw a close-up of barbed wire. She was mesmerized by the harshness of it. She was drawn to it and it touched her. It symbolized exactly how she felt inside, like she was trapped behind barbed wire. No one could come in and she wasn't coming out.

The ache in her heart intensified until it burst like a dam and tears began to stream down her cheeks. The pain she routinely pushed down reared its ugly head again and the familiar voices in her head spoke such ugliness over her, coming in waves of disgust. Annmarie felt nauseated and ran to the bathroom.

She sat on the bathroom floor and blurted, "How did my life get so awful? How could you take away my parents, God? How could you do this to me? My family was good! They were the only ones who ever really truly loved me. You took love away from me! I'm nothing! Nothing! Nothing! No one wants me. I'm a nuisance. I'm fat and ugly! Who would want me?! My life is a joke!"

She wallowed in her sea of bitterness for a long while. Then, exhausted, she dragged herself back to her bed, laid her heavy head on her pillow and fell fast asleep.

Annmarie found herself in the same wooded area from her first dream. This time she noticed a line of trees and a little pond. She looked down and realized her feet were bare again—not at all fazed by the cold of the snow.

She carefully scanned the winter-like landscape, hoping to catch a glimpse of the ruby red cardinal again. She spotted the hill she had climbed before and decided to hike up its terrain again. As she climbed higher, the snow faded away. Grass was growing and daffodils were sprouting up everywhere. She turned and saw the cave again and bam— there it was! The jeweled cardinal beamed bright and proud. It seemed to stare into Annmarie's soul. She smiled and greeted the bird, "Hi Ruby!"

As she tried to reach for her gem, Ruby playfully soared to a higher tree branch—out of arm's length. Annmarie wished she could fly away, too. She turned her attention back to the cave entrance. It looked very dark and dismal inside. She peeked her head in and reflexively clenched her face tight as she felt a strong breeze hit her—

Annmarie opened her eyes to see Paul standing over her, blowing hot air right into her face.

Disgruntled, Annmarie shoved him hard. Paul started laughing. "What's your problem? I was sleeping!" Annmarie scolded.

"Hey, you were breathing so heavy, I came in to see if you were okay—you weirdo!" Paul laughed. "What's for dinner, A?"

Annmarie pulled herself together and stomped into the kitchen. "Frozen pizza. Do you want cheese or pepperoni?"

She was still fuming.

"Pepperoni, duh!" Paul teased back. He loved getting her riled. It was easy for him to get a rise out of her.

Annmarie turned the oven on and waited for it to preheat. She turned around and barked, "Get to your homework, right now. Your mom's orders!"

Paul instead laughed and turned on the TV. "I'll get to it after dinner." He stretched out his body to fill the couch and put his hands behind his head.

Annmarie was so irritated that Paul had thwarted her dream. She loved that she had visited the same place again. It was the first time she ever remembered going into the same place in a dream twice! Ruby was so vibrant and seemed almost supernatural. Annmarie crossed her fingers and hoped that she would dream of the magical destination the next time she fell asleep.

Chapter 5

Annmarie popped the pizza into the oven and scooted Paul over so she could sit down on the couch, too.

"Paul don't ever wake me up like that again. How many times do I have to tell you to respect my privacy?" Annmarie scolded.

"Whatever. You should be thanking me, A. I could've saved you from dying in there. What's the big deal?"

"Just don't." Annmarie retorted.

They turned on the TV and watched *Little House on the Prairie* together until the timer went off to indicate the pizza was cooked. It was an old show, but Annmarie enjoyed the stories. Watching a family who loved one another so much, even in the face of hardship, made her feel envious, but peaceful at the same time.

For some reason she couldn't explain—and one they would never talk about or admit to one another—Paul seemed to enjoy it as well. Oddly, they had an unspoken agreement that neither one would ever snitch on the other for being closet fans of the show. Annmarie just didn't talk to people, and she suspected Paul knew that if he told anyone, he would only be incriminating himself!

Annmarie served up the pizza. She gave Paul two big slices and put only half of one on her own plate. She was pretty hungry but also determined to lose weight. As they dug in, there was a loud crash outside the door.

Annmarie rushed to the door and tried to look out the peephole to see what was going on. She couldn't see anything, but then they both heard a faint cry for help. Annmarie and Paul looked wide-eyed at each other, before Paul leapt off the couch and joined Annmarie at the door.

As Paul opened the door, they looked down the hall and saw Ms. Opal on the stairs. She had fallen and her bags of groceries were strewn about the stairwell and hall.

"Oh, thank goodness!" Ms. Opal moaned as they rushed over to help. "Help me honey, will ya?" She grasped Paul's hand as he assisted her into a seated position, resting her back against the wall.

"What happened, Ms. Opal?" Annmarie began to gather scattered groceries.

"I tripped, and I think my knee is bleeding. Do you think you could run and get me a bandage?" Ms. Opal breathed in sharply through her teeth. "I'm not going to try to move just yet."

Annmarie ran back to their bathroom and rummaged frantically through a drawer looking for band-aids. She finally found a few in a box, collected a roll of paper towels while she was at it, and ran back to the staircase. Paul had continued picking up the scattered groceries.

"Thank you so much, kids. I don't know what happened. My knee hit the stair really hard, though." Ms. Opal sounded like she had regained her composure.

Annmarie handed the paper towels and bandages to Ms. Opal who immediately started dabbing her bleeding knee.

"I think my guardian angels were looking out for me!" Ms. Opal shook her head and grinned. "I think I'm going to be just fine. Just a dandy of a scrape. I thought it was much worse. Annmarie dear, would you help me get up? Paul if you could just keep picking up those groceries and carry them for me, that would be such a help."

The kids felt relieved as they helped Ms. Opal into her apartment. She was hobbling and leaning on Annemarie.

"Okay, sweeties. Come on in. You're in luck, loves! I made chocolate chip banana bread this morning. Please help yourself to some and, if you don't mind, cut me a piece, too!" Ms. Opal sat on a kitchen chair and nursed her wound.

"Oh, Annmarie, honey, could you go in my bathroom and grab a little antiseptic cream?" Ms. Opal asked. "I sure don't want an infection. Gotta slather that on my scrape to clean it out good."

"Of course, Ms. Opal." Annmarie raced into her bathroom. She quickly opened the bathroom closet door and found a little wicker basket filled with first aid supplies. Ms. Opal had all kinds of ointments, bandages, creams, sprays and gauze.

A sign hanging on the inside of the closet door caught her eye. It had a snow-covered white birch tree with a bright red cardinal perched on a branch. Annmarie couldn't even believe it. *What are the odds?* As she looked closer, she noticed a quote written on it:

"I am always with you."

"Seriously?" Annmarie laughed and shook her head. *Another cardinal?* Her dreams, the print in the laundry room, and now this sign. She imagined Ruby was following her! Could all of this be more than coincidence?

"Annmarie, dear, are you having trouble finding that cream? I have a little basket in the closet." Ms. Opal's voice snapped Annmarie back into reality.

"I found it. I'm coming!"

She returned to the kitchen and gave Ms. Opal the cream. Paul had already cut up some banana bread for them. It smelled scrumptious. Of course, he looked like Cookie Monster from Sesame Street as he ate.

"Ms. Opal, you make the best stuff," he mumbled while stuffing his face.

"Well, thank you, Paul. I do make a mean banana bread, if I do say so myself." Ms. Opal belly laughed as she watched Paul devour it. "My goodness, child. Take a breath. There's more where that came from!"

"Thanks, Ms. Opal," said Annmarie as she, with a bit more restraint, dug into her own serving of scrumptious dessert. "I'm so glad you are feeling okay. You scared us!"

"Oh sweetie, I'm quite alright. Thank the Lord! A little scrape will heal up in no time. Next time, I'm going to have to get help when I have so many bags of groceries. I need to slow my roll a little bit." Annmarie and Paul chuckled at Ms. Opal's slang.

Annmarie wanted to ask her about the cardinal sign hanging on the inside door of her bathroom but wondered if it was hidden for a reason. Most people hang their pictures on the walls for everyone to see.

"I'm so glad you kids were there for me or I might still be on those stairs. Annmarie, honey, are you okay? You look a little puzzled. Is everything alright, dear?"

"Oh yeah. I'm fine!"

"Hmm. Well, you know you can talk to me about anything." Ms. Opal said with a wink.

"Thanks." Annmarie loved it when Ms. Opal played the role of such a mothering figure.

"Well, Ms. Opal, we should get back to our place. Paul has homework and so do I."

Paul sighed in disgust.

"Okay, sweeties. Thanks again. Please take the rest of the banana bread. It makes a wonderful breakfast in the morning and you kids need your energy for school! I'm good now. Really, I am." Ms. Opal got up from her seat to reassure them she could walk just fine on her own. She grabbed Annmarie and Paul, gave them big mama bear hugs and sent them off with the bread.

Back in their apartment, Paul resumed his position on the couch and finished eating while watching TV. Annmarie put the rest of the banana bread on the kitchen counter and sat down next to him.

Suddenly, a wave of emotion hit her. She started to cry but didn't know why. Was she caught up in the emotion of seeing Ms. Opal on the stairs in pain? She tried to suppress it because she didn't want Paul to see her cry, but the tears didn't seem to care.

Paul looked at Annmarie with dismay. "Why are you upset? Everything is fine! Ms. Opal is fine. Everything is fine, A."

Not a little embarrassed, Annmarie jumped up, and snapped, "Just do your homework!" and darted to her bedroom, slamming the door behind her. She flopped on the bed and sobbed, still not even knowing *why*.

After the tears subsided, she gathered herself together and decided to distract herself by searching cardinals online. Maybe learning more about them would tell her something about why she was having these dreams.

She read that cardinals represent HOPE.

She also found it very interesting that cardinals mate for life and are good parents. The male shares in the responsibility of parenting. The call of the cardinal is cheerful and unique to gain attention and lift people up from depression or sorrow. The name for cardinal is rooted in the word *cardo*, meaning heart.

Annmarie smiled as she discovered how wonderful these birds really were. Not only did she realize that she absolutely needed a strong dose of hope in her life, she was reminded of the role lacking in her life that cardinals would seem to perfectly fill. Her parents had cared for her that way.

Although she realized it wasn't uncommon to like birds, Annmarie's fondness for this particular species was growing the more she learned about them. She wondered if Ruby was a sign that the healing she so desperately wanted was coming? The pain of loss, rejection and self-hatred had continuously tormented her to the core.

"God, if you are out there, please help me." Annmarie whispered.

Paul tentatively knocked on the door. "Annemarie? I forgot my homework in my locker. Can you walk me back to school to get it?"

The momentary hope she had been feeling vanished in a wave of irritation. "Paul, are you joking right now? It's really late. The school is closed up. There's no way you'll be able to get in there now. It's too late!"

"Aww, come on, A! If you don't go with me, I will go alone, and mom will find out!" Paul begged through the closed door.

"If you leave this place and go to school alone, you will be in big trouble!"

"But I have a big project due TOMORROW, and I need to get my stuff tonight! My grade really depends on this." He really didn't want to go to school alone, but he was desperate.

Annmarie jerked the door open to find that he had even started putting on his coat.

"Paul. Seriously. If you would have started working on your homework when I told you, we could have walked back to school, and the custodian would have been there. I'm not in the mood for this!" Annmarie crossed her arms over her chest and glared at him.

"Pleeeeeease, A! I will promise not to wake you again when you are sleeping. I really need to get my homework."

He looked at her with pleading, puppy-dog eyes.

Annmarie released a deep sigh and relaxed her arms as she relented. "Okay, fine. I doubt we will be able to get in there, though. Grab a flashlight—and wear your hat!"

As Annmarie and Paul walked to the school, Annmarie noticed smoke coming out of many chimney tops. She wished she could be comfy and cozy next to a hot, crackling fireplace. She added a fireplace to her list of "someday," where she and her dog would cuddle up at night and just be happy. She daydreamed about the design of her future home.

As they approached the school, they noticed the custodian stepping into his car to leave. Paul started running toward him, arms flailing like a lunatic. "Please stop, sir! I need to get to my locker!"

The man turned around and looked at Paul and shook his head. "I was just leaving for the night."

"Sir, please. I forgot my very important homework in my locker that I need to work on for tomorrow. My grade depends on this. I don't know how I forgot it! Please, sir?" Paul pleaded again. He was winded and on an adrenaline high, yet still managed to pull off the puppy-dog gaze once more.

Apparently, Annmarie wasn't the only one susceptible to the charms of a twelve-year-old boy. "I will do this for you this one time, but you better be quick. I need to get home," the custodian huffed.

"Great! Thanks, sir!" Paul beamed and followed him into the building.

Annmarie stood in amazement. She was honestly jealous that Paul always seemed to have favor with people. Everyone liked him—peers and adults alike. How did he do that? It wasn't fair. No one ever noticed or cared about invisible Annmarie.

Annmarie sat on a bench waiting for Paul and looked up in a tree. Two silly squirrels were playing and chasing each other up and down the tree trunk. They were having a blast together. Squirrel BFFs. *Even squirrels have friends to hang with.*

Paul had grabbed his books and came out of the school. He thanked the custodian with a high-five and jogged over to Annmarie who was in the middle of another pity party.

"Hey, A. What's the deal with the face? Look! I got my stuff!" Paul said proudly.

"Yep." Annmarie rolled her eyes at him.

"You know, A, you should really try smiling once in a while. It wouldn't hurt you." Paul urged playfully.

Annmarie wasn't amused. She stood up and started walking home. Paul followed her and then passed her as he pretended to be on a basketball court to shoot the last second shot for the win. He was cheering and patting himself on the back for a job well done.

Just then a driver honked. Paul and Annmarie turned around to see Jonathan Walters driving past them. Jonathan Walters was a junior, a star athlete, and very popular. He slowed down to give Paul a thumbs up. "Nice shot, bro!" Jonathan said as he chuckled and sped off.

"Thanks J-Walz!" Paul laughed back.

"J-Walz? Paul, how do you know him?" Annmarie asked.

"Oh, we're tight! The high school did a basketball clinic and we got to play with the varsity team. He was on my team and he's, like, the best player, and he's so cool!" Paul replied with a gigantic grin.

Secretly, Annmarie had always admired Jonathan because he was popular yet still seemed nice. It didn't hurt that he was really attractive, and all the girls wanted to date him. He had short, wavy brown hair and the bluest eyes you ever saw. They literally sparkled. He was tall and athletic. She liked to watch him from a safe distance, knowing she was nowhere near his league. Just being around him made her palms sweat.

"Why, Annmarie?" Paul taunted, doing his best impression of a girl swooning over a boy. "Do you like him?"

"Shut up, Paul!" Annmarie pushed him and started marching home more quickly.

Paul started laughing. "Yes ma'am, Mrs. Walters!"

Annmarie turned around and started chasing him as he ran at top speed, laughing hysterically. Suddenly, she felt like one of the squirrels she had been watching earlier.

"Paul, I am never going to help you again if you don't stop!" Annmarie shouted. As she shouted, a snowball hit her square in the face. For a split second, they both froze in shock. He hadn't meant to hit her in the face, and Annmarie had a mouthful of snow. She wiped her face and started running at top speed at him. He booked it home, screaming all the way.

He dashed into the apartment and locked the door before Annmarie reached it.

Annmarie pounded on the door with her fist. "Paul, open this door right now!"

"No way!"

"YES way!"

"I will only let you in if you promise not to hurt me. I'm sorry! I didn't mean to hit you in the face, A!" Paul whimpered.

"Fine." Annmarie answered.

He very slowly opened the door, but as she darted after him, he retreated to his mom's room and shut the door.

Abandoning the chase, Annmarie ran into the bathroom to wipe off. Her heart was pounding, both from exertion as well as the thought that someone may have heard what Paul had said. She was petrified at the idea of a rumor starting about her liking Jonathan. She could already hear everyone laughing at her.

As she exited the bathroom, Aunt Bonnie walked in and asked, "Where's Paul?"

"He's in your room." She was so glad they had made it back before Aunt Bonnie.

"Paul, why are you in my room?"

Paul peeked out the door and cautiously crept into the living room. He glanced at Annmarie who glared back at him.

Paul answered, "I don't know."

Aunt Bonnie shook her head and told Paul to stay out and finish his homework. He immediately obliged.

"I'm so tired. Glad they let me go early. Is there any leftover pizza?" She looked in the kitchen and saw their plates with partially eaten pizza still on the table. Grabbing a piece of pizza, Bonnie said, "Annmarie, clean up this mess and finish these dishes. Why can't you remember to do these things? I'm tired of telling you to help out."

"Mom, while we were eating, Ms. Opal fell on the stairs and we had to help her. She hurt her knee really bad." Paul tried to come to Annmarie's aid.

"Yes, then she gave us some banana bread. It's on the counter over there." Annmarie pointed out as she rushed to the table to clean up.

Aunt Bonnie sighed and put her pizza in the microwave. As she was eating, she received a text from her mom:

> Bonnie, Your father and I were wondering if you and Paul and Annmarie were available next week? We will be in the area Thursday and thought we could take you all out for dinner. Love, Mom

Bonnie looked at her calendar, hoping she had to work that night. To her dismay, she was not scheduled, so she didn't have a good reason not to meet her parents. Bonnie still deeply resented them because they hadn't been there for her and had forced Annmarie on her after Janet died.

"Your grandparents are in town next Thursday night. Do you guys want to meet them for dinner? I may have to call in to work and see if they can use me. I don't want to go," Bonnie huffed.

Paul and Annmarie looked at each other smiling. Going out to eat was a luxury for them, and they didn't care who was taking them.

"Oh, wait. Pauly, you have basketball practice Thursday," Aunt Bonnie pointed out as she scanned the calendar on her phone. "Sorry, bud."

Paul sulked and whined. He really liked good food and eating out. He could eat a whole pizza in one sitting and follow it up with a 3-scoop ice cream cone. He was always hungry.

"I'll go," Annmarie offered happily. "I don't have any activities."

"That's fine. But if I do go into work, you will have to make sure you are back here before Pauly gets home from practice."

Annmarie's grandparents would occasionally call out of the blue to meet for dinner. They would also generally bring a gift to relieve their guilt of not being there. Annmarie liked the gifts and the dinner, but she had never felt close to them.

"Why do they think they can just weasel their way into our lives only when it's convenient for them? They have a picture of us at home—they should just visit that. The nerve," Bonnie grumbled with disgust.

The moment Bonnie said the word "picture," Annmarie remembered she had her photography assignment due. She had no idea what she was going to take a picture of that would be good in black and white. She needed something with contrast, and she wanted it to look like she put some thought into it. Something interesting.

Chapter 6

The next morning, Annmarie woke up and pulled the covers over her head as the alarm sounded out its harsh call. She was bummed that she couldn't recall her dream. She wondered if she was going to see Philly again on the way to school. The thought made her uneasy.

Paul burst into the room and jumped on Annmarie. He was a get-up-and-go kind of kid, even though as a night owl he would stay up late and fall asleep watching the TV. Although the two of them had shared a room since he was a baby, and the bedroom contained two twin beds, Paul's bed was the couch. He kept his belongings in the room but had "moved out" into the living room when he was ten. Aunt Bonnie hadn't been thrilled with this arrangement and had tried and tried to get Paul back into the bedroom. However, as always, Paul got his way. Annmarie was fine with it because she needed her own space.

"Get up, A!" Paul shoved Annmarie.

"Stop, Paul." Annmarie shoved him back.

"Will you make me pancakes this morning? I'm sick of granola bars. They are boring. Please?" Annmarie glared at him.

"Listen, Paul. You are twelve years old. Why don't you make breakfast for us today?" She actually would love pancakes, but she didn't want to make them, mostly because Paul was badgering her.

Paul shocked Annmarie by leaving abruptly. Usually he would badger her until he got her upset. He really knew how to push her buttons.

Annmarie finally got up, grabbed a shower and got dressed. She could smell something burning in the kitchen. She ran in to discover that Paul had tried to make pancakes himself. A very bad idea. Annmarie started fanning the smoke detector because she was afraid that Aunt Bonnie would wake up and scream.

"PAUL! What are you doing? Turn off the stove right now!" Annmarie scream-whispered at Paul. Her eyes grew wide as her stomach churned with fear.

Paul had dripped heaps of batter onto the burners and all over the stovetop, causing the smell and smoke. He had never been allowed to cook at the stove because Bonnie still treated him like he was six years old.

Paul fought back frustrated tears. "I'm sorry, A. I just really wanted pancakes, and I knew we didn't have much time before school. I am really hungry! I was going to share with you."

Annmarie threw a rag at Paul and told him to wipe up the spill. Annmarie opened a window and crossed her fingers that the smoke smell would not stay.

"Paul. You've got to stop and think. You've never made pancakes before. I can teach you if you ask your mom if it's okay. Don't ever do something so stupid again! If she wakes up, we are in so much trouble." Annmarie scolded.

Miraculously, they were able to clean up the mess and get out the door to school before Bonnie woke up. They left later than usual, so Annmarie wasn't sure if she would run into Philly or not. Her stomach was tied up in knots as they ran to school. She hoped that Aunt Bonnie would not notice the smell of burnt pancake batter.

Not in the mood to listen to her babble, Annmarie was relieved to see Philly way ahead. Her mind returned to guilt-ridden thoughts about the pancake fiasco and the potential consequences if they were found out. Regardless of it being Paul's idea, she knew she would get the brunt of the blow. Aunt Bonnie had creative ways of punishment, too. Annmarie remembered the torment of having to scrub the entire bathroom floor with a toothbrush. She cringed at the thought of having to do so again.

On top of all that, her photography assignment was due. She took her school camera so she could take some pictures outside during lunch break. She crossed her fingers, hoping to find an interesting treasure in the midst of her boring, mundane, gray surroundings. She looked around at the bare trees and slushy, dismal landscape. It was overcast as usual, and it made the air feel thick and heavy.

Before she knew it, she was opening the door at school, and suddenly, out of nowhere, Philly jumped in front of her. Annmarie practically jumped out of her skin as she let out a scream of which any horror movie director would be proud.

"Boo!" Philly laughed as she poked Annmarie in the shoulder. "How are you? I saw you were a little behind today. Thought I would surprise you. I'm good at sneaking up on people!" Philly said proudly.

Annmarie felt a little nauseous.

Philly giggled and ran off waving. "See you in photog."

A moment later, Janice walked by, pushed Annmarie from behind and whispered, "Boo," in her ear, laughing nastily along with others who were nearby.

Annmarie groaned, gathered herself together and ran to class with tears in her eyes, overwhelmed with embarrassment and frustration with her morning so far.

The day seemed to drag on. Annmarie couldn't seem to concentrate in any of her classes because she felt sick to her stomach. She had forgotten to eat breakfast or pack a lunch because of the pancake fiasco. Fear tightened its boa constrictor grip on Annmarie. It was an all-out assault on her today.

Thankfully, she survived her morning classes and made it to lunchtime. Annmarie grabbed her coat, camera, and a pass to leave the building, kindly supplied by Mrs. Smith. She was relieved to grab some fresh air and snap a picture for her project that was due. As she walked around, she saw a bunch of naked trees and bushes. There were icicles on the school building, the sign, and on the cars in the parking lot, but nothing seemed really interesting.

Annoyed at the lack of material, Annmarie sat down on a bench in front of the school and carefully scanned her surroundings for any surprises. She closed her eyes in frustration. She had waited too long, and now she would have to make do with a boring photo.

Suddenly, she heard a bird chirping that she hadn't noticed before. She opened her eyes and looked up into the sky. Initially, she didn't see anything, but she followed the sound around the building. Her heart skipped a beat when she saw a bright red cardinal perched on a branch, singing as if it hadn't a care in the world. Annmarie fumbled with her camera and was able to get a few shots of it before it flew away.

"WOW!" Annmarie blurted out with exhilaration and relief, as a grin brightened her face.

She walked back into school feeling like a new girl. She was so refreshed and excited that she forgot she was starving. What were the chances that a cardinal would be right there at that moment? She was starting to feel like Nancy Drew, solving an unexplainable mystery.

Philly darted over to Annmarie as they battled their way through the halls to their photography class.

"Hi, Annmarie! So, what did you photograph for the project?"

"A bird."

"Oh, that's cool! I took a picture of this really cool lamp post near our house. It's kind of old-fashioned looking. I also took some pictures of my dog, Chewy. I'm hoping at least one of them processes well! By the way, the yearbook committee is pretty cool. You should really think about coming," she suggested with an exaggerated wink.

Annmarie methodically shook her head no.

Philly laughed. "Annmarie, you are funny."

Annmarie raised her eyebrows and looked at Philly like she was crazy. That was a new one. No one had ever thought she was funny before.

Before Annmarie could reply to Philly's ridiculous comment, Mrs. Smith spoke up and asked if there were any kids that still needed to process their assignments. Half the class still needed to process their film in the dark room, and only four students could process at a time.

"We will take turns processing film into negatives, class. If you aren't in the lab with me, you can be studying the notes we've been taking for the test we will have tomorrow. If you are not able to get in the lab in class today, I will stay after school and you can do it then," Mrs. Smith offered. "We need to get all the film processed today."

Mrs. Smith called kids into the lab in alphabetical order by last name. Annmarie sighed because with a last name of Williams, she knew she would have to wait until after school. Annmarie sulked because she really wanted to process her film right away. She was actually excited about her cardinal pics.

Mrs. Smith called out the first four names and they went into the darkroom lab.

"Annmarie, do you want to study together?" Philly asked.

"Um, okay." Annmarie answered.

"I sure hope we get time in the lab during class today," Philly said. "I have another Yearbook committee meeting after school. I know you aren't really interested in joining, but it really is fun."

"I'm sure it is," Annmarie responded sarcastically.

The girls got out their textbooks and quizzed each other on the test material on black and white photography history and different methods of processing negatives. The room was buzzing with activity. Many of the kids were talking about how excited they were about the pictures they shot.

After forty minutes, Mrs. Smith called out the last four names: "Philomena Phillips, Jack Rolf, Jason Sandborn and Sadie Strutz. This will be the last group to go during class. If you haven't gotten a chance yet, you are welcome to stay after school."

Annmarie was perturbed.

The final bell rang. Frustrated, Annmarie took out her phone and decided to scan Instagram while she waited for her turn in the lab.

Moments later, Philly bounded out of the lab with a big smile on her face. "Annmarie, the lab is so fun! It's really dark in there. At first, I put my hand in front of my face and I could hardly see it! It takes a while to get used to the darkness. I'll see you tomorrow morning on the way to school, unless you decide to join us tonight in the cafeteria later. We are meeting until 5:15pm."

Annmarie laughed sarcastically. *Fat chance!*

The majority of the class left, leaving Annmarie with one student from her own class and two others from Mrs. Smith's earlier class. Annmarie's palms began to sweat when she saw Jonathan Walters. Immediately, she looked down at her phone as her heart started racing. *Play it cool, girl. Just breathe!*

"Okay class, this works out very well. You are the last four to work in the lab. You have plenty of time to process your film," Mrs. Smith said happily.

Jonathan sat down and looked at Annmarie. "You look familiar."

"Who, me?" Annmarie answered him but couldn't quite meet his eyes.

"Yeah. You were walking with Paul last night, weren't you?"

"Oh, yeah. He's my cousin." Her heart was jumping out of her chest and she could hardly breathe. Holy Cow! Jonathan was talking to her!

"You were out pretty late last night."

"Yeah," Annmarie smiled awkwardly, finally attempting to meet his gaze.

"Paul is a pretty good basketball player. He'll do well here next year," Jonathan gave her a smile, as though he were telling her it was okay for her to speak.

But, as Annmarie found herself mesmerized by his sparkly blue eyes, she had no words. She was melting.

Annmarie was thankful to be snapped out of her trance as Mrs. Smith ushered the four remaining students into the dark photo lab to process their film. All the equipment they needed was in the darkroom. The first step was to let their eyes adjust to the darkness and then pop the film out of the casing. Annmarie was having a difficult time getting the film out and she sighed heavily as she worked at it.

"Do you need some help?" She recognized Jonathan's voice.

"Um, yes." Annmarie said. She felt his hand on her shoulder.

"Here, give me your film."

Annmarie handed it over.

Jonathan popped off the top for her and gave it back.

"Thanks J-Wal...I mean, Jon...I mean..." Annmarie stuttered.

"No problem." Jonathan chuckled.

It wasn't easy getting the group's film into the canister for the chemical bath, but she finally worked it in. Once the group was all set, they stepped out of the photo lab and laughed as they covered their eyes to adjust to the bright light. They went to a different part of the classroom where the chemicals and water were stored. They poured the chemicals and the water into the canister and agitated it on and off for about eight minutes. Then they took the film out of the canister and hung the processed negative rolls up to dry in a special dryer just for film.

Annmarie was so proud that she could see the pictures of the cardinal she had taken in the negatives. She couldn't wait to have the actual pictures in hand. That cardinal had saved her miserable day.

"What's that?" Jonathan asked, looking over her shoulder and pointing at Annmarie's negatives.

"Oh…it's a bird," Annmarie answered nervously.

"Looks like a cardinal. The Cardinals are my favorite baseball team. Nice choice."

"Yes! It is a cardinal." Annmarie was amazed that he could tell. She wanted this moment to last forever. Jonathan standing there talking to her. Oh, if only she could stuff this moment in a bottle and take it out every day!

"See ya later, Paul's cousin," Jonathan said with a wave.

"Annmarie." She blushed.

Jonathan gave her the guy head nod of approval and headed out the door. Annmarie flopped down at a nearby desk because her legs were limp spaghetti noodles. She was dizzy as her mind played back the entire scenario. She couldn't believe Jonathan had talked to her, helped her and even touched her shoulder! It wasn't even just because he was popular and probably the most beautiful boy she'd ever seen. There was something about him that set him apart as being different. She couldn't quite put her finger on it, but she again felt like she was in a dream world! Elation catapulted her into the stars.

Just then, her stomach grumbled, and Annmarie realized her dizziness may not have been just because of her encounter with Jonathan but because she hadn't consumed any food or beverage all day long.

Mrs. Smith tapped Annmarie's shoulder and gave her a thumbs up. "You did a great job in there, Annmarie. I hate to push you out, but I have to close up shop and get going."

"Okay, Mrs. Smith. Thank you."

Annmarie packed up her backpack. She practically floated home. She didn't even care at that point about starving or even if Aunt Bonnie had found out about the pancake mess. She had had such a beautiful afternoon. What had started out to be one of her worst days had become one of her favorites.

Chapter 7

The night came for the dinner date with Annmarie's grandparents. Paul couldn't be there, and Aunt Bonnie couldn't get hours at the hospital to avoid it, so she and Annmarie went to an Irish pub nearby called O'Donoghue's. Grandpa Eli and Grandma Em had specifically chosen this restaurant.

On the way, Bonnie nervously fidgeted with her hair.

"Okay, Annmarie. We will tell them we can't stay long because we have to get Paul from basketball practice." She looked down at her phone while they were stopped at a stoplight. "So, we have about forty-five minutes to eat and get out of there."

Annmarie nodded. Paul had a key to the apartment, so they really didn't have to hurry to get home or pick up Paul from practice. It was just an excuse. Only if it was an emergency would they pick him up from school. That's it. Otherwise, he walked home with a group of players who lived nearby.

45

Even if it were only for a short time, Annmarie was really excited to be going out to eat. Although she was serious about losing weight, she felt justified in giving herself a cheat day and order whatever looked good to her. She had been so good at starving herself. She deserved a break!

As they entered O'Donoghue's, they saw Grandpa Eli and Grandma Em already sitting at a table enjoying their beverages. Grandpa Eli excitedly waved them over to the table. Bonnie sighed and sauntered over with an overtly annoyed look.

"Hi. We're here but we can't stay long. Gotta get Paul from basketball practice in forty-five minutes or so," Bonnie blurted out as she took off her coat and sat at the table.

"That's fine, Bonnie. I'm glad you were able to meet for dinner tonight." Grandma Em beamed, ignoring the obvious disinterest and disdain Bonnie conveyed. "And how's our sweet Annie?" Grandma Em asked, looking at Annmarie.

Annmarie smiled and nodded. "I'm okay."

"You sure are growing up fast, Annie!" Grandpa Eli said as he left his seat to give her a little side hug.

The waitress came to the table, welcomed them and gave them menus. She asked if they wanted a beverage and rattled off their choices.

"We need to order quickly because I have to leave here in about forty minutes. So, if you could be back to take our order pronto that would be great, and you'll need to expedite our order. I'll have a ginger ale." Bonnie commanded.

The waitress raised her eyebrows and gave a sarcastic grin in response to Bonnie's harsh and demanding tone. She then looked at Annmarie.

Annmarie ordered a Diet Coke and quickly scanned the menu. She saw they served Reubens. That was easy! She loved Reubens and French fries. She wished they had more time to stay because there was a dessert called "Bub's Bread Pudding" that looked fantastic. Annmarie was really enjoying the uplifting, fun Irish music playing in the background, too. It offset Bonnie's mood perfectly.

"Well, we have some news to tell you. Your father will be retiring soon, and the firm wants to give us a going away vacation. The president of the company has gifted us with a getaway in Ireland! They are giving us a house for a week and we were wondering if you and Paul and Annie would like to come?"

"You've never invited us before," Bonnie said sourly. "Why now?"

"Bonnie, I know I was gone so much because I poured myself into work. Now that I'm retiring, I realized that I'm entering a new freedom to enjoy more time with my family. We're excited to share this with you," Grandpa Eli explained.

Aunt Bonnie stared off into space.

"Bonnie, we've had some time to reflect on life and what is most important to us. We had this great idea to go to Ireland together to help us really reconnect with you and the kids," Grandma Em tried to clarify.

Bonnie laughed out loud. "Seriously? What's the catch? I don't really know what to say other than I've done just fine without you, and I don't really need or want to reconnect with you." A heavy blanket of ugly unrest enveloped the atmosphere.

The waitress came back with the drinks and set them down before Bonnie and Annmarie. They all ordered their food. Annmarie could feel the waitress squirm in the tangible thick, dark cloud looming over the table. After taking the orders, she scooted out of there as fast as she could.

"We understand you're upset Bonnie, but we are trying to make amends. Ireland in March is beautiful. Spring is a time for new beginnings. What do ya say?" Grandma Em tried to sprinkle a little hope on the situation.

"The kids have school and I work. There's no way we can go. This is foolishness," Bonnie retorted.

"We have spring break in March," Annmarie shared hopefully. Annmarie longed to get away. She had never really traveled anywhere, let alone to another country. Not only that, but her birthday was in March. It would be amazing. She could bring her camera and take some A-plus quality pictures for class.

A glimmer of hope sparkled in Grandpa's eyes. "We could take the kids for you during spring break, Bonnie. That would give you a break?" Grandpa Eli said.

"I don't know…" Bonnie said, twirling her hair.

Annmarie knew that Aunt Bonnie would be thrilled to be completely free from the kids for a week. That never happened. She was battling this internally. If she said yes, she would have given into them. If she said no, she would have the kids all week.

"Well, please consider it, Bonnie," Grandma Em said. "We will need to get passports for you all if you come, and that can take a few weeks. I don't want to rush you, but we will need to know in the next few days."

Annmarie looked at Bonnie pleadingly. Bonnie looked away, staring at her phone and refused to engage further with anyone else at the table. Annmarie was so frustrated with her intolerance. She understood Bonnie's pain in feeling abandoned, but she couldn't understand why she would throw such a tantrum. This was really the chance of a lifetime!

"Annie, how are you doing? How is school?" Grandma Em asked, deciding it would be best to change the subject for a bit.

"Okay. I'm taking a photography class."

"Oh, sweetie. Your mom had such a good eye for photography. I bet you have a bit of that in you, too. She was so creative—such a gift to share." Grandma Em's eyes glistened with tears. Grandpa Eli put his arm around her and quickly changed the subject again.

"How is Paul doing? Is he still playing basketball?" Grandpa Eli asked Bonnie.

"Yes," Bonnie answered without looking up from her phone.

"Oh, he has such talent for sports. He is a lively one, isn't he, Annie?" Grandma Em pulled herself together as she looked at Annmarie.

"He's something," Annmarie answered with a laugh, trying to lighten the mood.

The food came quickly, as Bonnie had requested, and everyone ate in silence. There was a little small talk here and there, and despite the mood, the food was delicious. When it was time for Bonnie to leave, she got up, put on her coat and without saying a word started walking to the door. Annmarie scrambled to get herself together to follow Bonnie.

"Bonnie, you go ahead and get Paul. we can take Annmarie home so she can finish her meal." Grandpa Eli said. "Then we can pop in and give our boy a quick hug, too."

Bonnie turned around and looked at her father, looked at Annmarie, shrugged her shoulders and kept walking.

"Relax and finish your meal, Annie. We want you to enjoy it." Grandma Em patted Annmarie on the arm. She was surprised that Bonnie hadn't forced her to come along.

"Thank you," Annmarie whispered. She took a deep breath as the black cloud rolled out the door with Bonnie. She was so happy to get to stay and finish her meal.

"We sure hope you can come, Annie. We'd like to spend some time with you," Grandma Em said. Annmarie could feel their authenticity.

Annmarie wanted to forgive and move on, but she was afraid of getting hurt again. She was afraid of Aunt Bonnie and how it would affect her home life. And she was emotionally exhausted.

"Hey, Em and Annie, this looks good. Do you want to get Bub's Bread Pudding for dessert?" Grandpa Eli asked.

"Yes!" Annmarie blurted out. "How did you know I was looking at that?"

Grandma Em laughed at Annmarie. "I think we are all on the same page here, lassie!"

They called over the waitress again and politely asked for Bub's Bread Pudding and for another Reuben and fries to-go, for Paul.

When they finished, Grandpa Eli paid the waitress, gave her a big tip and apologized for Bonnie's behavior. The waitress smiled kindly and gave them the to-go bag.

They got to the apartment and knocked on the door. Paul's footsteps could be heard racing to the door. He opened the door and invited them to come in. Grandpa Eli handed Paul the bag of food and his eyes lit up like a Christmas tree. He unwrapped it immediately and scarfed it down as though he hadn't eaten in days, as usual.

"Did your mom talk to you about anything special?" Grandma Em asked.

Paul wiped his mouth and shook his head.

"Em, you should probably wait and let Bonnie talk to him first. We don't want to step on her toes, dear." Grandpa Eli said, knowing that Em wanted to invite him.

"What?" Paul asked.

"You'll find out soon," Annmarie assured him.

"Where's your mom?" Grandma Em asked Paul.

"She went to the grocery store."

"Oh, I see. Well, your mom has some big news for you when she gets home, doesn't she, Annie?" Grandma Em said.

"Well, give us a hug, Mr. Paul!" Grandma Em said as she and Grandpa hovered over him as he was eating. He stopped to get up and hug them, and then they left.

After they left, Paul looked at Annmarie as he continued to gobble his food. "What was that about?" He mumbled.

Annmarie nonchalantly shrugged her shoulders.

"Come on, A!" Paul pleaded while chewing.

"Can't tell you," Annmarie said with a smile. It was fun flaunting a secret.

Just then Bonnie walked into the apartment with some groceries. "Help me with these. What in the world are you eating, Paul?" Bonnie asked.

"Food from Grandma and Grandpa!" Paul answered.

"Of course." Bonnie rolled her eyes and threw her keys on the table.

"Mom, what's the big news?" Paul asked.

"I bought more frozen pizzas," Bonnie said.

"What? Grandma Em and Grandpa Eli said you had news for me," Paul said, wiping his mouth with his shirt sleeve.

"Don't wipe your mouth with your sleeve, Paul," Bonnie scolded, throwing a napkin at him.

"They are going to Ireland. Grandpa is retiring and they're going on a trip again. Not a big deal."

Annmarie stared at Bonnie wondering if she would tell Paul they wanted him to go, too.

Paul shrugged his shoulders because it was not a surprise that they were traveling. "That's it?"

"Well, they invited us to go during your spring break but I'm not sure if that's a good idea or not," Bonnie said as she put groceries away.

"Wait. Ireland? Like, where four-leaf clovers grow and leprechauns live? The real Ireland?" Paul asked. His voice climbed a higher octave in excitement.

"I'm pretty sure. You don't have a passport, you've never flown before, and you would be away from me for a week because I can't take off of work for that long," Bonnie said as she tried to dissuade him. "I could sign you up for basketball camp instead."

"Mom. I want to go. Can I go? Please? I've never gone on a trip like that!" Paul pleaded jumping up and down. "I can get a passport! It will be fun! Will A go, too?" Paul's pleading eyes were wide, as he put his puppy-dog decision converter to work, yet again.

Bonnie couldn't resist Paul's persistence, either. If there was one person who could persuade Bonnie of anything, it was Paul. It didn't hurt that the thought of being alone for a whole week really appealed to Bonnie, too.

"Well, I guess. I don't have extra money for passports, so your grandparents will have to take you to get that taken care of," Bonnie huffed.

Paul looked at Annmarie and shouted at the top of his lungs with excitement and even lunged at Annmarie for a hug. You would have thought he won the lottery!

"I'll text them and let them know to get you tickets and passports," Bonnie said. "And, settle down! Both of you, get to your homework right now."

They obliged and crashed their books on the kitchen table. Annmarie didn't normally study anywhere near Paul, but this was a special day.

Paul smiled at Annmarie and whispered, "Dude!"

Annmarie couldn't help but agree.

That night, Annmarie had a hard time falling asleep. She had looked up Ireland on the internet and found masses of photos of green hills, stunning countryside, castles and sparkling blue water. She had never been so excited in her life!

She was extremely anxious about flying, but that would not deter her! Her desire to escape trumped the fear, for now. Annmarie was banking on magical Ireland to renew her hope and give her a new perspective. She was also stoked about taking some amazing pictures!

Finally, her mind wound down to a crawl and Annmarie fell back into dreamland.

She found herself right where she had left off before, at the mouth of the cave on the hill. She looked around and saw Ruby in the tree to her left gazing at her. She peeked into the cave, and it was dark and smelled musty.

She stepped inside and as her eyes adjusted to the dim light, she saw carvings on the cave walls: birds, a large Celtic cross, and a door with flowers carved right where a door-knocker would normally hang. As soon as her eyes saw the door carving, a breeze blew in with an explosive floral scent. She closed her eyes and breathed in the sweet aroma which released a feeling of ecstatic joy. The smell was overpowering, yet she couldn't get enough of it.

She looked around to see where the fragrance was coming from, but she couldn't see anything in the cave that could be the source. She turned around and wandered back outside, squinting as her eyes adjusted again to the sunshine. There were a few flowers here and there but nothing that could produce such a strong perfume.

As a matter of fact, the smell dissipated as soon as she was outside. It made no sense. Confused, she walked back into the cave and again waited for her eyes to adjust. However, now the intoxicating scent was completely gone. *This is really strange.*

She decided to walk into the cave a little further to explore, but the further she went in, the darker it got until she couldn't see her hand in front of her face. She sighed with delight as she remembered her darkroom encounter with Jonathan at school. She turned around and walked back to where she could see some light. She sat on a boulder near the cave door and just looked around.

Suddenly, she heard a rich voice say, "See what I want to show you. Unlock your heart and walk through the door."

Annmarie was surprisingly unafraid of the voice. She thought to herself, *I don't know what I'm looking for.*

She heard the voice again, "I will help you find it."

The sound of a chirping bird woke her. She looked at the clock, which again (just like after her first dream) read 2:22AM. She turned on a light and rummaged through her nightstand for a pen and notebook. She wrote down what the voice in the dream had told her and spent the rest of the night replaying the dream over and over in her mind until she finally drifted off to sleep once more.

She woke up in the morning feeling unusually awake and full of energy—a far cry from tired, cranky and bitter, which is how she usually felt. She always wished to go back to sleep, but today was different.

Paul banged on Annmarie's bedroom door. She politely gave him permission to come in. Paul eased opened the door, bursting to ask her a question, yet cautious due to her unusually good mood.

"A, would you, um, please make some pancakes for breakfast?"

"Sure, Paul. Let's do it together," Annmarie answered.

Paul looked at her incredulously. "...Really?"

Annmarie nodded. "I don't want to have a mess like we had before. And besides, pancakes sound pretty good."

Paul cheered.

Annmarie showed Paul how to read the directions on the box of pancake mix, how to add the eggs and oil and mix them together. She showed him how to pour just a small amount on the buttered griddle.

"Maybe we could put some green food coloring in the pancakes for Ireland!" Paul said.

"You could do that, but I think that's weird. Do you remember in elementary school when we would have Dr. Seuss Day and they would give us green eggs and ham? Ew!"

"YUM!" Paul disagreed. "I love it!"

Annmarie rolled her eyes. She showed him how to flip the pancakes at the right time. "You have to wait for bubbles to form on top. Then you know they are ready to be flipped."

Paul did just as Annmarie showed him. "Hey, I think I got this! This is fun!

"Maybe Mom will let me use the stove to make pancakes again if you're not around. Maybe I could bring her some breakfast in bed!" Paul suggested.

"Your mom really likes her sleep. Just leave some out for her to eat later," Annmarie said. "I'll get out the syrup and butter. Finish flipping those last pancakes and put them on this stack. We can eat at the table."

They ate their pancakes together at the small table and talked about Ireland and how excited they were to get away on a vacation.

"I'm geeked to get away, even if it is with old people we hardly ever see," Paul grinned.

"I'm just looking forward to getting away from here for a while."

They finished eating, left a pancake stack on the table for Bonnie and got ready for school.

Paul and Annmarie met Ms. Opal in the hallway on their way out. She had her hair coiffed nicely and she looked like she was going somewhere special. It was unusual for them to see each other so early in the morning like this.

"Hi, Ms. Opal! Where are you going?" Paul asked.

"Oh loves, good morning! I was invited to a lady's group at the church this morning. Can I give you a ride to school on my way out? I'm guessing that's where you are headed. I will be driving right past there," Ms. Opal offered cheerfully.

Paul and Annmarie looked at each other and smiled. They never turned down an offer for a ride to school.

"Dude! Yes! Thanks, Ms. Opal!" Paul exclaimed.

They walked out the door together, and Ms. Opal started singing "You Are My Sunshine" as they entered the parking lot. They were happy to see that the sun was peeking out from behind the clouds.

They piled into Ms. Opal's red Ford Fiesta. As they hooked into their seat belts, Ms. Opal asked them if they knew why she decided on a Ford Fiesta. The kids shook their heads.

"Did you know that the word fiesta means party? I want to drive through life and see it all as a celebration. Red is such a bold color, too. It stands out. Every one of us is a one-of-a-kind stand out. That includes you two," Ms. Opal shared. "It's going to be a good day!"

Paul nodded in agreement. Annmarie smiled, even though she thought it was ridiculous. She admired Ms. Opal but really felt like she was unrealistic. She was in her own little Ms. Opal world. Annmarie's truth was a far cry from a celebration. However, today did feel lighter and happier for some reason. Maybe it was the pancakes or the connection with Paul. Maybe it was the ride to school or the sunshine.

Ms. Opal turned the radio onto a 1950's station. "Mr. Sandman," a song about dreaming, happened to be playing. Annmarie was amused, and reminisced about her special, secret dream all over again. She could almost smell the flowers.

Ms. Opal graciously let them out in front of the middle school doors. She waved her hand frantically at them as they left, wished them a blessed day and sped off down the road.

Annmarie walked over to the high school. Because Ms. Opal drove them, she was really early. She was happy to not have to be in a hurry. From a distance behind her she could hear Philly calling to her.

"Hey, Annmarie! Wait up!"

Annmarie turned around. Philly was jogging toward her waving her arms. Out of breath, Philly laughed and asked Annmarie why she was so early. Annmarie explained she had gotten a ride.

"Aha," Philly said. "That's cool. Hey, I was wondering if you wanted to hang out for a while after school today. We don't have any meetings for Yearbook. Wanna come over and meet Chewy? We could do homework or something. My mom made her famous oatmeal chocolate chip cookies last night. They are the bomb!"

Annmarie was speechless. She hadn't been asked to hang out with anyone for years. She was afraid. Paul had practice after school so she didn't have to wait for him, and Bonnie wouldn't be home. She usually went home, did some chores and homework and watched TV alone. There really wasn't any reason she couldn't go.

"Um, I'm sorry, but I have to go right home…"

Through her disappointment, Philly suggested, "Maybe another day?" Annmarie didn't reply. She certainly didn't want to hurt Philly's feelings, but she just wasn't ready to dive into a friendship. Like a turtle in danger, she retreated back into her tiny shell for protection. She waved, shot Philly a quick half-smile, and rushed to her locker. She didn't even see as Philly smiled back and turned to walk to her own locker.

The school day seemed to fly by more quickly than usual, as Annmarie had Ireland on her mind. When she got to her photography class, she noticed Philly was already sitting and waiting for her. Annmarie sighed quietly and walked toward her.

Mrs. Smith lectured the class about travel photography. Toward the end of class, she presented them with a new assignment. She wanted everyone to take a series of three or four pictures over spring break that would represent a different culture. It could be a person or a landscape or even foods. The pictures had to represent something and along with the photos they had to write a paragraph describing the culture they were capturing and why they chose it.

She then asked the class to raise their hands if they were traveling for spring break. A slew of hands went up, but Annmarie couldn't bring herself to do the same. Mrs. Smith called on each one to share about their destinations. There was someone going to Hawaii. Many were going south to Florida or Texas. When you live in Wisconsin, the winter is a time to escape to warm weather.

"For those of you going somewhere new, this will be fun. For those of you staying in town over break, you may have more of a challenge—but we actually have many cultures right here in our city. Think about restaurants or specialty grocery stores. This assignment may open your eyes in a new way to the diversity right here in Milwaukee," Mrs. Smith said.

"We're just hanging around here. I guess I'll be challenged with this assignment," Philly whispered to Annmarie. "Are you staying, too?"

"Actually, I'm going to Ireland with my grandparents," Annmarie whispered back.

"Why didn't you raise your hand?" Philly asked. "That's really cool!"

Annmarie shrugged her shoulders. *Doesn't she get it?* Annmarie thought to herself. *Is she blind? Can't she take a hint? Doesn't she see that I just want to fade into the background? Why does she keep talking to me?*

Mrs. Smith noticed the girls whispering back and forth and asked in front of the class if they had any questions about the assignment.

"No, Mrs. Smith. Sorry to interrupt. I was just asking Annmarie about her trip to Ireland," Philly said.

The whole class turned around in amazement and stared at Annmarie. She turned a shade of tomato red and began sweating profusely, her heart beating like a timpani drum. She honestly thought she might actually pass out from embarrassment.

"Why, Annmarie! That is an exciting destination! Ireland is a beautiful place. I've never been there myself, but I have seen pictures. I'm sure we will get a whole new perspective when we see yours," Mrs. Smith said with a smile and a wink.

The students all turned back around and gathered their belongings as the bell rang.

"Have a great weekend, kids," Mrs. Smith announced. "Have fun planning those spring break trips!"

"Wow, Annmarie. That is going to be an amazing trip. I've never been outside the country," Philly squealed.

"Neither have I," Annmarie said. "I have to get a passport this weekend."

"Well, I'll walk home with you today since I'm not staying after," Philly said.

"Oh, well, I'm not allowed to have anyone over without my aunt there," Annmarie said. "And she is never there when I get home."

"Oh, I just meant until I have to turn off toward my house," Philly said. "I wasn't inviting myself over. I wouldn't do that."

Annmarie breathed a sigh of relief.

"However, you are always welcome at my house. My parents have the same rule, but my mom is always home after school because she hasn't found a job yet. She told me that she would look for something part-time when I'm in school so she can be home when I'm home. She really likes to cook too, and her cookies are the best."

Annmarie nodded her head. She had a strong urge to roll her eyes. It sounded like Philly had the perfect family, complete with a mom at home and a dog. She was drowning in a sea of jealousy.

What would Philly want with a misfit orphan like herself? No, this friendship was a lost cause. She knew that she would always feel inadequate, resentful and just plain jealous.

"Okay," was all Annmarie could muster up.

The girls started walking out of the school together, and the sound of Philly's voice drifted into background noise. Philly was relentless in trying to connect with Annmarie, and she didn't understand why. Annmarie stubbornly blocked her out. Either Philly was crazy or just plain strong-willed.

The girls parted ways. Annmarie nodded and they waved goodbye to each other. Walking home alone was all that she wanted. She lost herself in daydreams of Ireland. Getting away couldn't come quickly enough!

Chapter 8

The day had finally arrived! Paul and Annmarie's grandparents picked them up outside of their apartment. After loading Grandpa Eli's SUV, they said goodbye to Aunt Bonnie, piled in, and set off.

"We are on our way! We are really going to do this! Aren't you excited?" Grandma Em enthused. "We are really looking forward to this adventure, aren't we Eli?"

"Yes, dear. It really is going to be great. I can't wait to eat corned beef and cabbage rolls!" Grandpa Eli responded, patting his jolly belly that was wedged beneath the steering wheel.

The drive from Wawatosa to Chicago O'Hare International Airport was only about an hour and a half long. Annmarie was beyond excited to get away but still felt a little unsure about the airplane ride. She was thankful for Paul's non-stop chatter, as he was beside himself and convinced that leprechauns were not only real but that he would encounter one on the trip.

Upon arriving at the airport, Grandpa Eli parked in long-term parking and they made their way into the terminal. After checking in, they promptly went through security to get to their gate, and after sitting down, Grandma Em asked if anyone wanted a snack from the little gift shop across from the gate.

"Oh yeah! ME!" Paul answered. He never rejected an offer for food. "Hey A, wanna come?" Paul asked.

"Okay," Annmarie answered, even though she really wasn't hungry. She was feeling nervous about flying, but she thought the walk to the shop would distract her from her queasy stomach.

The shop had magazines, chips, candy, drinks and souvenirs. Paul grabbed a big bag of chips, a Coca-Cola and a bag of sour gummy worms. Annmarie looked around at the souvenirs and found some stylish journals. She thought it might be kind of fun to get a journal for the trip. She was drawn to one with Midwestern birds on it. A bright red cardinal was right in the center. Annmarie smiled. Before she could even ask Grandma Em if she could get it, Grandma Em snatched it out of her hands to take to the cash register.

As they walked back to the gate, Annmarie thanked Grandma Em for the journal.

"I could see a twinkle in your eyes as you were looking at it, dear. I remember your mom had that same twinkle in her eyes when she saw something she liked. It was my pleasure to get it for you," Grandma Em said.

Emotion flooded Annmarie's heart as she listened to Grandma Em compare her to her mom. How she wished she still had her parents with her. It was refreshing to hear someone speak about her because Aunt Bonnie never did.

"Do you think I look like my mom?" Annmarie asked.

"Yes, my dear. You have your own look, but I can see your mom so clearly in you," she replied. "Your mother would be so proud of you."

Annmarie smiled warmly as her Grandma put her arm around her shoulders and gave her a side squeeze. "Let's make up for lost time, Annie. I'm looking forward to getting to know you so much better on this trip."

Annmarie was deeply touched at Grandma Em's words and gestures but was still unsure of her intentions. So, as usual, she guarded her heart.

They walked to the gate to settle in and wait for boarding. Annmarie took out her boarding pass just to make sure the ticket said "Ireland" and not "Russia" or "Timbuktu." She still had a suspicion that this dream trip was some kind of April fool's joke! But, sure enough, it said Flight 222, bound for Cork, Ireland.

Well, that looks pretty real.

As boarding was announced, Paul and Annmarie glanced once more at their boarding passes to find their seat numbers: 22D for Paul and 22E for Annmarie. Paul rubbed it in that he got an aisle seat, but she was just focused on trying not to throw up. She was still nervous about her first flight.

Grandma Em and Grandpa Eli sat with each other a couple of rows behind. Because the flight was an overnight trip, the stewardess gave everyone a pillow, blanket, and an eye mask to help them sleep.

"A, I am so pumped that we are here right now!" Paul said, spraying chip crumbs all over Annmarie.

"Seriously, dude. Ew!" Annmarie said, wiping herself off.

Paul laughed and the chips sprayed even more.

A large man came to sit on Annmarie's right side. As he greeted her, Annmarie noticed he had a thick Irish accent which reminded her that they were *really* going to Ireland!

The take-off was smooth sailing, but Annmarie was still nervous. She tried to remove all fear of crashing out of her mind but couldn't seem to shake it. Her heartbeat accelerated and she felt increasingly sweaty and more nauseated. Her chest tightened as though a python had her in its grasp. As it became harder for her to breathe, she grabbed onto Paul's hand with a panicked death grip.

"HEY! A, what's wrong? Let go—that hurts!" Paul whined.

In contrast, with his impressive size, the man seated next to her asked gently, "Are ya alright, lass?"

"I've never flown before," she gasped and began to cry. She tried to focus on her breathing, but the tears kept coming. Paul's eyes were wide and beginning to fill with tears of his own, either from empathetic concern for his cousin, or simply the pain of having his fist crushed.

The man's face practically oozed compassion and assurance. He made a gesture to the stewardess and asked her to bring Annmarie a ginger ale. He then delicately extricated poor Paul's offended hand from her clenched fist and took her other hand in his own instead.

"Don't worry, lass. This plane'll make it safely to Ireland. I've flown this way hundreds of times. I assure ya, there's nothin' ta worry about." He gave her hand a comforting squeeze. "My name is Patrick, but you can call me Paddy, if ya like. Go ahead and breathe. The flight'll be grand." His voice was like a calm, steady stream.

Grandma Em unbuckled her seatbelt and came to see what all the fuss was about.

"Annie, what's the matter, dear?"

Annmarie was unable to respond.

"Grandma! A is *freaking out*!"

Patrick gave Paul a little shush and addressed Grandma Em, "Don't worry, she's gonna be just fine. She's just gotta get used to the idea of flyin' is all!" He gave Grandma Em a charming grin as he punctuated his words with more comforting taps to Annmarie's death grip.

Although her face was still clouded with worry, Grandma Em couldn't help but return Patrick's smile with her own. Turning to Paul, she said, "Paul, dear, go take my seat next to Grandpa." She replaced Paul next to Annmarie to try to comfort her.

Patrick continued to encourage Annmarie from one side, while Grandma Em stroked her hair on the other. The stewardess brought the ginger ale and added the reassurance that she had been working for the airline for twenty years and had always flown safely.

Finally, Annmarie was able to loosen her grip on Patrick's hand. He winked at her and said, "There's a good lass. I'm proud o' ya! Maybe I won't lose my hand after all!"

She responded with a weak chuckle. *I'm not dead, yet. Maybe this'll be okay!* Grandma Em offered Annmarie a dose of melatonin, which she gladly took with her ginger ale.

"Just relax, close your eyes, and lay your head on my shoulder, Annie. All you need is a little rest." Annmarie obeyed as she hiccupped her subsiding tears into rest. As she leaned against her grandmother's soft shoulder, she was so thankful for her support when she had needed it. Before she knew it, the steady sound of Grandma Em's breathing and the gentle hum of the engines had lulled her into sleep.

Annmarie found herself in her cave once again. She noticed the same boulder she had used for a chair, the same etchings on the walls and the same damp earth beneath her feet. She could feel the cool moisture and a tingle went through her legs. There was an excitement coursing through her, yet in this cave she felt safe and protected.

She heard Ruby singing outside. Drawn to the melody, she peeked her head out of the cave to see if she could spot her majestic bird-friend. This time she noticed, to her surprise, the bare trees that had been there before were now green and full. The intensity of the new colors caught her off guard. Contrary to the snowy setting of before, yellow and purple wildflowers were now sprinkled throughout the lush carpet of emerald grass surrounding the outside of the cave.

Clearly a shift of season had happened from winter to spring. The sky was as blue as a peacock feather, and fluffy white clouds happily floated along. She marveled at the transformation of this world. She noticed there were many different birds and butterflies flitting around the area but had yet to spy Ruby.

Annmarie tiptoed out of the cave and walked closer to the nearest row of trees. Ruby's whereabouts weren't as easy to detect as before due to the fullness of the leafy branches. Ruby popped her head out playfully as if to welcome Annmarie.

The sun shone brightly on her face. Annmarie could smell the same sweet floral scent she had noticed before and she knew it was the sweet wildflowers releasing their perfume. She had never seen such beauty in her life—it was all too perfect and lovely.

She felt such tranquility, she decided to sprawl out on the blanket of grass to ingest the heavenly scene in all its brilliance. As she lay there blissfully, she felt a tugging at her hair. She laughed as she turned to see a squirrel playing with her ponytail.

Suddenly, she woke from her dream with a twitch.

"I'm so sorry, honey. You were sleeping so peacefully I didn't want to wake you up, but the stewardess came by again with drinks. I must've accidentally brushed against your head to get my tea."

Annmarie smiled as she rubbed her eyes. Since she was right there, the stewardess asked Annmarie if she would like a beverage and she agreed to another ginger ale.

Annmarie's blissful state lingered as she woke up. She felt that these were no ordinary dreams but wondered what they could mean. Could this be something supernatural?

"I'm so glad you were able to get some good shut-eye, Annie. You were asleep for a few hours. I think you needed it. You actually look like you're feeling much better," Grandma Em said.

"I do feel better." Annmarie yawned. She finished her ginger ale and laid back against her Grandma Em. Patrick shot her a quick wink and a thumbs up.

Chapter 9

The airplane landed in Cork, Ireland. Annmarie was so relieved to have landed and was grateful that her grandma, Patrick and the stewardess had been so kind to her in her anxiety.

"I'm proud o' ya, lass! You enjoy your time here in Ireland!" Patrick said. "T'was a pleasure sittin' with ya both."

Annmarie nodded her head and thanked him for helping her to which he assured her that she was a trooper.

Paul made a beeline to her and hugged Annmarie as hard as he could.

"Annmarie, you freaked me out! Don't do that ever again," Paul scolded. Annmarie gave him a gentle squeeze in return, in spite of her minor annoyance. He could be a really sweet kid…sometimes.

They went through customs and security and collected their suitcases. Grandpa Eli hailed a taxi to take them to the seaside cottage where they would spend the next seven days.

The weather was cool, and the sky overcast, yet the charming old stone cottage was quaint and delightful, nestled in the rocky hillside, overlooking the water. A stone walkway leading to the front door was accented with multi-colored tulips and bright, golden daffodils in full bloom.

An elderly couple came out to greet them as the taxi drove away. The woman's silver hair was styled in a short bob, and the gentleman's salt and pepper hair was partially covered by a tweed golf cap.

The pleasantly plump woman warmly greeted them first. "Welcome to 222 Meadow Lane! My name is Erin O'Leary, and this is my husband, Ian."

"How ya doin'?" Ian chimed in, as he reached to help carry their baggage. "How were your travels?"

Grandma Em glanced at Annmarie, and they exchanged a knowing smile, before she answered, "We had a lovely flight."

"Except Annmarie got weird on the plane! We thought she was going to be sick!" Paul's eyes widened dramatically as Annmarie rolled her own with a small, yet exasperated sigh.

"Oh, sweet one! I'm so sorry," Erin directed her full attention to comforting her new guest. "Well, let me assure ya that our cottage doesn't fly and everyone who stays here has an enchantin' time! You'll enjoy your time here, love."

Annmarie nodded and smiled as Erin and Ian led them into the old, yet lovingly restored, three-bedroom cottage. The aroma of fresh bread baking in the oven filled the house.

Annmarie could feel the history of the old place and noticed the low ceilings and narrow staircase. There was a cozy wood fireplace just like she had always dreamed of having.

The kitchen's bright, lemon-yellow walls were accented with a wallpaper border of lovely pink flowers, and the living room featured a large picture window, providing them a beautiful view of the water outside. A large farmhouse dining table held freshly cut, happy daffodils in a crystal vase seated on a handmade doily. There was a bottle of red wine on the table for Grandma and Grandpa, and Erin brought out homemade iced tea for the kids.

Ian and Erin shared about the cottage and different activities the family could engage in during their visit. They took turns describing the most appetizing local restaurants and pubs, a nearby golf course, a bike rental shop, and the best places to go fishing or sailing. Erin beamed as she told them of the beautiful walking paths nearby.

She then gave them a thorough tour of the home and showed them every nook and cranny. Annmarie loved the inviting and peaceful atmosphere, and the whole property embodied tranquility and beauty—it was so different from their tiny apartment. Rest and relaxation were definitely on the agenda!

Annmarie was especially excited about seeing where her bedroom would be and followed Erin up the steep stairs, followed from behind by Ian lugging some of the suitcases. Erin showed Grandma and Grandpa the room they would stay in. It was the biggest room with a queen-sized bed, decorated in a blue and white nautical theme, complete with an anchor hanging on the wall and a model ship on the dresser.

Next, Erin explained that there were two other bedrooms available, each with twin beds. The first room was very plain, with a heavy, multi-colored patchwork quilt on the bed that looked well loved.

"My mother made that quilt many years ago—it's my favorite!" By Erin's nostalgic smile, it was obvious that she cherished it as a family heirloom.

The second bedroom was painted Kelly green and the bed was clothed with a floral comforter. Matching watercolor paintings of sunflowers and daisies hung on the walls.

"These are originals." Erin gestured toward the artwork. "In the summer, I love to garden, but I'll set up my easel an' paint the flowers, too! It gives me so much joy to capture their beauty on canvas to enjoy forever." She paused and gave Annmarie a secretive wink, "What do ya think, love?"

Paul didn't even wait for Annmarie to answer. "I'll take the patchwork room, Ms. Erin!" he insisted. "You're good with the flowers room, right, A?"

Annmarie chuckled at his excitement and obvious boyish aversion to flowers. "Yes, that works for me." She wasn't sure why Erin's wink seemed to imply some sort of shared conspiracy, but she was happy to stay in a room surrounded by these watercolors. The flowers were so life-like it was almost as if they were blooming right in front of her eyes.

"I'm so excited to have my very own room, A! This is sick, bro!" Paul shouted, as he ran across the hall to his own room to settle in.

"Oh dear. Are you feelin' ill, Paul?" Erin looked concerned.

Annmarie laughed. "No, Ms. Erin. When something is 'sick,' it actually means it's really great."

"Oh my. Well your family is 'sick' then!" Erin exclaimed with a hearty chuckle.

Everyone laughed.

They walked back downstairs and made their way to the farmhouse table. They all sat down together to review the house rules and to answer any questions over the fresh bread, iced tea and wine.

"My daughter Lily will swing by mid-week ta check in with ya. She'll be bringin' her daughter, Kennedy, with her. She's fifteen years old. How old are you, Annmarie?"

"I'm fifteen, too." Annmarie answered.

"And I'm twelve!" Paul chirped in.

"Our Kennedy is so sweet and adventurous, and she loves hikin'. If you are up for it, she may like ta show ya some of the paths around the area," Erin suggested.

Annmarie was less than interested in making friends with a strange girl from Ireland. She had no intention of going anywhere with any stranger. She would be just fine on her own, but she nodded in agreement with Erin to appease her. Annmarie was already scheming how she could make herself scarce when they came to check in on them.

Annmarie tasted the hot, fresh bread with butter that Erin baked, and it literally melted in her mouth. She couldn't hide the ecstasy on her face.

Erin giggled when she saw the bliss on Annmarie's face. "I see that expression often when I serve my great-grandmother's prized bread recipe. It's been in the family for generations. Her baking is what inspired me to start a bakery."

Annmarie smiled at Erin and the entire table giggled and nodded in agreement that the bread was scrumptious.

After a while, Ian commented that they all must be tired from such a long trip and suggested they relax and get a nap in if they needed. Annmarie liked that idea very much. Erin and Ian shook Grandma Em and Grandpa Eli's hands, gave a little hug to Paul and Annmarie, and promptly left.

The four stood in the hallway smiling at each other. They had just witnessed such wonderful hospitality and anticipated a nice, long nap. They had made it all the way to Ireland, and it was charming and inviting.

"Well, I don't know about you all, but I'm exhausted right now," Grandpa Eli said. "As soon as I heard the word nap, my eyes grew heavier than ever. I'm going to take one! Maybe in a few hours we could play some cards. I brought a few decks with me."

"Yes, we thought it would be fun to teach you how to play some games," Grandma Em chimed in.

"I need a nap, too." Annmarie answered with a yawn.

"I think I will sit in this armchair and read a little bit, Eli. I'll also check out the kitchen and see what may be available for us to eat later for dinner," Grandma Em said.

"Oh, Em. We can just go out to eat if you'd like," Grandpa Eli suggested.

"I'd like to eat in sometimes, too. I'll make a list of things we may need from the supermarket," Grandma Em answered with a wink.

"I don't really want to sleep. I'm going to check this place out and maybe go down by the bay." Paul said.

"Paul, I'd like you to wait on that. This is the rule: we are in another country, and we are responsible for you both. You are not to go anywhere outside this house without someone else with you. We can go and check out the bay together later as a family," Grandma Em said sternly.

Paul grumbled a bit, but ultimately agreed and decided to just explore the house and settle in, especially after he glanced outside and saw that it had just started to rain.

Annmarie walked up to her room and shut the door behind her. She opened her suitcase and put her clothes into the drawers. She found her fuzzy polka dot fleece pajama bottoms and a t-shirt to get comfortable in. She pulled out her camera and decided to take a picture of her bedroom.

It was her first picture in Ireland, and she was excited to take many more. She loved her room. The floral paintings on the walls were colorful and bright. Her comforter was very plush. The accents of lace on the edge of her pillow and on the dresser were very quaint and old-fashioned. She could live in this pretty house. She pulled the pink and green striped window panels closed to darken the room and fell into a deep, restful sleep.

When Annmarie finally woke up, she fully expected it to be only a few hours later, but when she looked at her phone, it was 3:30AM. She was wide awake! *This must be jet lag,* she thought. It felt like it was 8:30AM.

She got out of bed and glanced down the hallway to see if anyone else was awake. She tiptoed over to Paul's room, peeked in and saw him snoring away. Grandma and

Grandpa's door was shut. She wondered if they had gotten up and played cards or did anything fun earlier that night. She crept through the quiet house back to her own room and turned on a light.

Annmarie decided to take out the bird journal with Ruby on it that Grandma Em bought for her at the airport. She wrote the date on the top of the page and wrote:

March 24th

Ireland Spring Break Vacation

Dear Diary,

Today I arrived in Ireland with Paul, Grandma Em and Grandpa Eli. I was so afraid of flying, but a nice man named Patrick helped me breathe and ordered a ginger ale for me and Grandma Em helped me. I was able to snuggle with my Grandma. She might care about me after all!

I wonder why they brought us to Ireland. I don't understand. Bonnie always is angry with them because they don't care about us. I'm excited about taking pictures here and enjoying a fire in the fireplace. I'm excited to be away. The house we are staying in is so cute. My room is perfect. The bread that Ms. Erin served us today was the best thing I've tasted besides Ms. Opal's. This bread was amazing—warm with melted butter. Who knew plain old bread could taste like heaven? It's so nice here that I may have to run away so I don't have to go back home.

Annmarie closed her eyes and breathed in to see if she could still smell the bread in the air. Yes. Yes, she could still smell it. She *had* to get the recipe!

After writing in her journal, Annmarie didn't know what to do with herself. She decided to just close her eyes and try to fall back to sleep, but her body and her mind did not cooperate. She thought about Philly and wondered what she was doing back home. She liked Philly, but she was relieved that here she could avoid the pressure of trying to connect with a girl so outgoing and energetic. Being around

Philly could be exhausting! Then she thought about Jonathan. He was so wonderful! *I wish I was good enough for him.*

She had the "if only" virus, and it robbed her of joy and happiness. Even in this glorious Irish setting, the "if only monster" came to steal. If only she were prettier, thinner, smarter, wealthier, more loveable, more courageous—the list went on and on. Self-doubt always had a way of pushing the "if only" song button in her heart. When the virus struck, Annmarie shut down completely. She felt powerless against it. The dark and quiet house intensified her negative thoughts, and the same panic attack fear from the airplane slithered into her stomach and throat.

Her heart's tempo became more rapid. She immediately opened her eyes and sat up in bed, trying to breathe. She ran over to open the window to inhale fresh air. She was stunned at how fast the torment had overtaken her again. What was it? She started crying because she was scared. She scanned the backyard and tried to redirect her focus on the surrounding view.

It was still pretty dark out, so she had to strain to see. Everything looked dark and gray, but she could see flowers, trees, and hills and she heard birds chirping and water lapping in the bay. She took a deep breath and desperately tried to assure herself that everything was going to be okay.

Just then Paul knocked on her door. Annmarie looked at the clock to discover it was 4:30AM. Before Annmarie could answer, Paul burst into the room.

"Top of the mornin' to ya, A!" Paul greeted her with a truly awful attempt at an Irish accent. "I can't sleep. I heard you open a window in here, so I thought I'd come in and bug ya."

Annmarie didn't turn around to greet him because she didn't want him to see her coming down from a panic attack. Actually, his presence in the room helped her calm down.

"Can you please get me a glass of water?" Annmarie asked, without moving.

"Why?" Paul asked.

"Or some tea," Annmarie pleaded. She was hoping he would just leave and give her a minute.

"Let's go together. We can look into the fridge and see what they have." Paul came to grab Annmarie's hand. He gasped when he saw her face. "What's wrong with you? You look weird!"

"I'm fine. Let's go," she said with tears still welling up in her eyes.

"You're shaking!"

"I'm fine. It's just jet lag," Annmarie waved off his concern.

Quietly, the two of them rushed downstairs to the kitchen. Annmarie opened the fridge, found the iced tea and searched the cabinets for glasses. She asked Paul to pour because she was still shaking and afraid she might break the glasses or spill the tea.

They sat down with their drinks at the farmhouse table. Paul had a very serious look on his face. "Annmarie, you look like you're gonna hurl."

To the surprise of them both, Annmarie accidentally passed gas instead, which made them both laugh hysterically. Then Paul, who had a very special talent of being able to pass gas at will, forced out a grand fart that seemed as loud as a fog horn. They laughed so hard they were falling off their chairs. This time, tears were streaming out of Annmarie's eyes because she was laughing so hard.

"Aww, yeah! It stinks, too!" Paul shouted.

"Ew, Paul!" Annmarie pinched her nose in response.

Grandma Em flew down the stairs while tying her robe. She saw the kids in the kitchen and asked if everything was okay. She had heard the kids laughing and falling to the floor.

"We're fine, Grandma. We couldn't sleep anymore," Paul said. "Just so you know, Annmarie farted."

"Oh good! I was worried when I heard the commotion," Grandma chuckled. "I'm going to try to sleep some more. Jet lag stinks like a fart! We'll be on Ireland time sooner than you can pick a four-leaf clover."

As soon as Grandma Em reached the top of the staircase, the breath the kids had been holding back burst out in renewed hilarious laughter. Who knew their Grandma Em was so laid back about gas humor? Aunt Bonnie would have had a fit!

After their laughter had subsided, Annmarie shoved Paul for what he had said about her. "You stinker!" Annmarie accused.

"You love me," Paul proudly exclaimed.

Annmarie rolled her eyes and smirked. At least she felt the intensity of the fear lift, for now. She hated anxiety, but she was pretty sure she was in trouble. She'd always struggled with it, but it seemed to have kicked up a notch with the vacation.

By now it was after 6AM, and the sun was rising. Annmarie walked toward the window, looked outside and saw the sky, painted with orange and royal golden hues accented with pink, hugging the water. It was breathtaking and Annmarie motioned for Paul to come and see it for himself.

"Cool!" Paul exclaimed.

Annmarie ran as quickly as she could to grab her camera. She flew down the stairs and out the front door to take a snapshot of the awakening seascape. She took three pictures and heard a voice echo in her heart, "This is the dawn of a beautiful new day." Annmarie was taken aback by the words she felt rise up from inside of her. They brought her a measure of peace. She slowly removed the camera from her eye and soaked in the moment, inhaling the serenity.

Paul followed Annmarie outside, took a deep breath of the salty sea air and let out a deep sigh. "I'm going to catch some fish while I'm here."

"You've never gone fishing before."

"And while I'm fishing, I'm going to spot Nessie," Paul declared.

"What?"

"You know. The Loch Ness monster—duh!" Paul answered.

Annmarie laughed. "Oh, is that right? Is the leprechaun you are going to find going to show you where your Nessie is?"

Paul smiled proudly. "Maybe."

"Well, that's interesting. If you find your monster, what are you going to do with him? Catch him?" Annmarie decided to go along with this story to see where it would go. Paul was good at exaggerating.

Paul looked at Annmarie like she was ridiculous. "My plan is to find Nessie and get some good footage for my YouTube channel. I'll be on every talk show and make lots of money. I will be world famous and have enough money to ship Mom and all my friends here to live with us in a castle. Grandpa and Grandma would have to stay too."

"Hmmmm. I see. That's a plan. What about me? Would you want me to stay?" Annmarie asked.

"Well, J-Walz is my friend, and he'd obviously want to come here, too." Paul winked at Annmarie. "Then you two can get a house nearby together and live happily ever after."

Annmarie pounced at him. Paul shrieked and started running around the side of the house. Annmarie ran after him. However, as she chased Paul, she realized that she was still in her pajamas outside in public. So, she ran back into the house and locked the door so Paul couldn't get in.

Paul started banging on the door and screaming, "A, Let me in!"

Just then Grandma Em and Grandpa Eli raced downstairs to stop the madness.

"What is going on here?" Grandpa Eli asked. "Open this door, Annmarie."

Annmarie quickly opened the door. Paul and Annmarie looked guiltily at the floor.

"Kids, let's please keep it down. It is early here, and most people are still sleeping," Grandma Em said.

"Sorry," Paul muttered.

"Let's just try to be courteous, please. Are you all hungry? I saw some scones and fruit in the kitchen."

Annmarie and Paul were amazed. They had gotten off pretty easy compared to what would've happened back home. Bonnie would've been very angry and sentenced them to a heavy punishment. They were grateful for the grace.

After a delicious breakfast of Irish scones with blackberry jelly, sliced apples and hot tea, they all decided to get some fresh air and take a walk down by the bay. They all changed into some warmer clothes and coats and left to take a stroll.

The fishy sea smell tickled their noses as they drew nearer. There were fishing boats everywhere, and a farmer's market was set up under multicolored tents. They saw local vegetables, meats, wines, cheeses and apples as well as spring flowers, baked muffins, breads, artwork and jewelry. Grandma Em was pleasantly surprised.

"Who wants to join me at the market?" she asked them.

"I'll go," Annmarie answered.

"Grandpa, can we get closer to the water?" Paul asked.

"Sure, Paul. Sounds like a great idea. Have you ever gone fishing, son?"

Paul shook his head no.

"Well, we should see if a fisherman could take us out on a boat and give us a lesson this week," Grandpa Eli suggested.

Paul's face lit up with excitement. "Yeah!" Paul beamed.

Grandpa Eli smiled and gave Paul a high five.

"Em, make sure you pick up some yummy treats for later," Eli suggested.

Grandma Em looked at Annmarie and said, "Your Grandpa really loves his sweet treats."

Grandma Em and Annmarie visited nearly every booth, gathering all kinds of meats and vegetables. Grandma Em thought it would be nice if she made a hot corned beef dinner. She bought a variety of delicious snack foods as well.

Finally, they spotted a beautiful booth with the most extravagantly decorated cakes. "We should get one of those cakes!" Grandma Em exclaimed. Annmarie smiled and nodded in agreement.

A woman and her daughter stood nearby, manning the bakery booth. "Excuse me, we would really like to purchase a cake today," Grandma Em told the woman.

"Oh, hello, ma'am. Yes, of course. I'll wrap one up for ya. I see you aren't from around here. Are you visitin'?" the woman asked.

"Yes, we are staying over in a house owned by Erin and Ian O'Leary. We came in from the U.S. yesterday," Em shared.

"Yes, Hi!" The woman said with a big smile. "My name's Lily and this is my daughter, Kennedy," Lily said. "Erin and Ian are my folks. Pleased to meet ya!" Lily wiped her hands off on her apron and extended her hand for a handshake.

Grandma Em smiled and shook her hand. "Hi! My name is Em and this is my granddaughter, Annmarie. Erin told us you would stop by and check in on us."

"Yes! How's the form?" Lily asked.

Grandma Em gave her a very confused expression.

"How are you doin' at the house? Sorry, I have to remember to translate," Lily laughed.

"Oh, it's so nice, Lily. We love it."

Annmarie studied Kennedy as she boxed up their chocolate cake. She had the brightest red hair Annmarie had ever seen, half pulled back from her freckled face, with tight curls streaming down to her waist. Her eyes were a stunning pale blue. Annmarie was mesmerized by her striking features. Kennedy noticed Annmarie watching her and smiled warmly at her. Annmarie looked away, embarrassed.

"Annmarie, are ya sleepin' in the room with the flowers?" Kennedy asked.

Annmarie nodded her head.

"Ah! 'Tis my favorite room," Kennedy said.

"Well, we will be looking forward to your visit," Grandma Em said.

"Yes, we will wet the tea when we swing by," Lily said.

Annamarie and Grandma Em nodded and smiled and said thank you to Lily and Kennedy. They walked back toward the house and Annmarie glanced over her shoulder. She saw Kennedy waving, and quickly turned and looked ahead again, pretending she hadn't seen.

"Did you understand what 'wet the tea' meant?" Grandma Em asked Annmarie.

"I have no idea, Grandma. My guess is they want to drink tea together?"

"I imagine it's something like that, sweetheart," Grandma laughed along. "It's a whole different world over here, isn't it?"

"Yep," Annmarie agreed.

Grandma Em gave Annmarie a little side squeeze as they noticed Grandpa Eli and Paul standing together near the water. When Paul spotted them from the corner of his eye, his eyes lit with excitement and he ran as fast as he could toward them.

"Annmarie! Annmarie! We met a fisherman who said we could learn to fish on his boat. He told Grandpa that he wasn't a very good teacher but that we could use his boat tomorrow afternoon. Grandpa said he would teach me—or us if you wanted to come! Isn't that awesome?!" Paul squealed.

"That's really cool, Paul. You should enjoy a nice time together."

"You don't wanna come?"

"No." Annmarie answered plainly. She had a fear of being in danger of any kind, so fishing on a boat that could sink or tip over was definitely out of the question! Even worse, she dreaded the idea of another panic attack. If she was out to sea, what would she do?

Paul turned around and noticed Grandpa Eli had almost caught up to them. He was winded and breathing heavily but smiling as he continued up the hill toward them.

"Hi, Em!" Grandpa Eli said as he stopped to catch his breath. "Looks like we're going fishing tomorrow."

"Well, that sounds like fun, dear," Grandma Em smiled. "Maybe Annmarie and I will look for something else to do while you two are out. We could explore around the cottage or go into town."

Annmarie definitely preferred that idea. It might be fun to look at the shops and little cafés. She hoped she could find a nice souvenir, and she was sure there would be great photo opportunities, too.

But for now, Annmarie was looking forward to getting back to the cottage. She was starting to feel drowsy again, and began to feel like it might be time for a nap. Just the thought of sleep triggered a gigantic yawn. Grandma Em caught the yawn bug and had a nice long yawn, too.

Grandma Em chuckled. "Okay, that is our sign to go back and relax. Is anyone else up for a little nap? Jet lag can do that to you."

"I'd like a nap," Annmarie answered.

"No way!" Paul shouted. "I don't want to nap. I want to get ready to go fishing. Don't we need to get stuff like bait and poles, Grandpa?"

"I'm pretty sure our fisherman friend is well stocked, Paul. You sure are excited about this, aren't you?"

"Yeah, Grandpa! I've always wanted to go fishing!"

"Paul, son. I'm so sorry that it has taken us this long to go fishing together," Grandpa Eli said apologetically.

"Grandpa, it's okay. Thank you for bringing us here. This is awesome!" Paul said ecstatically.

Grandpa hugged Paul as tears pooled in his eyes. He was so grateful for the grace of a second chance.

Chapter 10

They all woke early again the next day as their bodies were still adjusting to the time difference. Grandma Em went right to the kitchen and discovered a treasure: a lacy retro apron with embroidered red rose buds. She couldn't help showing it off, prancing and spinning, giving a little fashion show to Grandpa Eli, Paul and Annmarie.

"Looking good, Em!" Grandpa Eli whistled.

Both Annmarie and Paul tried to copy the whistle but couldn't. Grandpa Eli tried to teach them but neither one could master it.

"Keep trying kids. You'll get it!" he encouraged.

Grandma Em returned to the kitchen to make homemade blueberry muffins and some yummy scrambled eggs with bacon cubes. The cottage smelled delicious and Annmarie couldn't wait to eat. It was rare that anyone made breakfast for her. Annmarie was so grateful that Grandma Em was happily cooking away in the kitchen.

"Good thing I'm not making breakfast," Paul glanced over at Annmarie and made a silly face.

Annmarie nodded in agreement, also remembering his pancake fiasco. It was a miracle Bonnie had never noticed.

"I just can't wait to go to fishing, Grandpa!" Paul blurted out. "When do we meet that guy again?"

"We meet him there at 10AM. We can eat quickly, play a few hands and then get going," Grandpa answered.

Grandpa Eli loved playing cards. His favorites were Golf, Sheepshead, Gin and Cribbage. He and Grandma Em played a variety of card games with friends on a regular basis.

Annmarie was warming up to her grandparents. They were displaying a kindness and love that was contradictory to everything her Aunt had told her. She wanted to trust them, but could she? Or would they hurt her like so many others had in the past?

"Annmarie! It's your turn!"

Paul's impatience snapped Annmarie out of her pensive thoughts, and she played her hand. Soon, Grandma Em was calling them to eat.

After a delicious breakfast, Grandpa and Paul left for their fishing adventure while Annmarie helped clean up the kitchen. Grandma Em hummed a happy tune that was unfamiliar to Annmarie. She even started to swing her hips as she plopped the dishes in the dishwasher.

Annmarie giggled watching Grandma's silly display. Never in a million years would Bonnie be caught singing in the kitchen.

At the sound of Annmarie's giggle, Grandma Em grabbed her hand and twirled her around a few times singing, *"You, my brown-eyed girl! Do you remember when we used to sing, sha-la-la-la-la-la-la-la-la-la-ti-da."*

"Grandma?" Annmarie laughed.

"Oh, honey. Don't you know this song? It's called 'Brown-Eyed Girl'—one of my favorites. It's a classic,"

Grandma explained as she continued to dance. "Brown eyes run in the family. You have those same big beautiful brown eyes, Anna Banana. Your mom loved calling you her Anna Banana."

Annmarie's laughter fell away, replaced by discomfort. She felt like her grandma was getting a little too personal, too fast.

"I'm gonna go shower and change."

"Oh, Annmarie. I'm sorry if I upset you." Grandma Em opened her arms to give her a hug, but she avoided her embrace, scooting quickly upstairs to her bedroom.

Annmarie vaguely remembered being called "Anna Banana" but it had been such a long time since she had heard her mom's pet name for her. Hearing it again triggered new waves of pain.

Annmarie closed the door behind her for some privacy. In frustration, she began making her bed, jerking the sheets into position. She wasn't angry with her grandmother, but it was difficult for her to navigate close relationships. She was conflicted, wanting so much to be closer to her family, yet afraid to open up.

She looked up at the ceiling, attempting to somehow see beyond the physical barrier into Heaven. "God, if you're real, please help me!"

Suddenly, a bird began chirping loudly outside her window. Distracted, she stopped and looked outside to find where the sound was coming from. A bright red cardinal was perched on her windowsill. She was in awe. Clearly, this must be a sign that He was listening.

She then noticed the bird journal that Grandma Em had bought for her at the airport laying on her pillow. As she saw the bright red cardinal in the center, she took a deep breath and smiled, feeling a wave of certainty come over her. She didn't understand why, but she knew that somehow God really was telling her that He was listening.

After she showered and dressed in a pair of blue jeans and an oversized sweatshirt, she gathered her courage and went to seek out Grandma Em. She looked all around the cottage, inside and out, but she seemed to have disappeared.

Did she leave without me? Annmarie thought, sadly. *Maybe she's disappointed. I bet she's even wishing they hadn't brought me to Ireland with them at all. I really blew it—as usual. What is wrong with me?*

Annmarie found a cute little white painted wooden bench in the backyard—a perfect place to mope and try to distract herself with games on her phone.

Annmarie heard the front door open and chatting and laughing voices: Grandma Em, Lily, and her daughter Kennedy. Annmarie hoped she could stay hiding in the backyard. She wasn't in a mood to socialize and she hoped they would leave soon.

"Annie!" Grandma called. "Annmarie? Where are you?"

Annmarie pretended not to hear and even plugged in her earbuds to make it seem legitimate in case her whereabouts were discovered.

"Maybe she's outside. It's a gorgeous day," Lily suggested.

Annmarie rolled her eyes and thought, *Of course.* Lily and Kennedy opened the back door and greeted her with smiles. Lily was holding a plate of homemade shortbread cookies.

"Hey, love! We saw your Nana out walkin' on our way to visit ya. We decided to bake ya some of my world-famous biscuits an' welcome ya proper!" Lily turned to Kennedy. "Cardy, won't you go in and put on the tea?" As Kennedy turned to obey, Lily looked back at Annmarie and insisted, "Come in and join us!"

Annmarie plastered a fake smile on her face and begrudgingly followed Lily into the cottage. They found Grandma Em in the sitting room.

Grandma Em smiled at Annmarie as though nothing awkward had ever happened between them. "Annmarie, while you were showering and getting ready for our afternoon together, I decided to walk down to the bay to see if I could see Grandpa and Paul, but they must've been further out on the water. That's when I saw Lily and Kennedy walking on their way to visit."

Annmarie glanced at the cookies, hesitantly. They looked absolutely scrumptious! *Should I?* Glancing quickly down at her body, covered up by the baggy sweatshirt, she thought, *I really do need to watch my calories...*

But...I would be rude to say no! So, telling herself she just didn't want to offend their guests, she grabbed a cookie. She took one bite and the delicate shortbread melted in her mouth! She couldn't resist and grabbed another one, placing them on a delicate china plate.

Kennedy carried in a tray with a matching fancy tea set, which she placed gently on the ornate wooden coffee table.

"Isn't this a gorgeous tea set? This is my mum's. She has such taste in finery," Lily said.

The china tea set was delicate and dainty, creamy yellow with a pattern of tiny pink and blue flowers all around the perimeter, accented by gold trim. Annmarie was pretty sure she had never seen, let alone used, such special plates and teacups. Not ever. She felt a little out of place using such opulent dishes.

"Cardy, would ya fetch the sugar and cream?"

"Sure, Mum," Kennedy hopped to accommodate her mother, curly red hair bouncing along behind her.

"Lily, I thought your daughter's name was Kennedy. Did I get it wrong?" Grandma Em asked.

"Oh, no, you're right! She's my Kennedy, but Cardy is my special nickname for her."

Grandma Em smiled and nodded her head, "I do love nicknames!"

Annmarie felt her face flush as she was reminded of the awkwardness of earlier that morning. She looked off into the distance, attempting to disengage from what struck her as an intimate topic of conversation.

Kennedy returned with the cream and sugar, placed them on the table, and plopped down next to Annmarie on the loveseat in the sitting room.

"Em, do tell us about yourselves," Lily suggested as she took out silverware for the tea.

"Of course! My husband, Eli and I have been very happily married for 47 years. We have worked very hard, and Eli and I both retired recently. He was a national sales manager for a manufacturer in the States, and he oversaw the sales team. He traveled constantly. I worked at a law firm, working way too many hours. To keep our marriage alive, I would take time off to travel with Eli." Em's face fell in regret. "As we prepared to retire, we realized that we had missed too much by working so hard, and we knew we wanted to catch up on our family relationships."

She shook her head, "It's a cruel joke isn't it? You work so hard to provide for your family and loved ones, but then you get so lost in your work that you inadvertently neglect the ones you love the most. Anyway, we were gifted this trip from Eli's employer as a retirement send-off, and we decided to invite our grandchildren to reconnect with them. Now we're here! Our daughter, Bonnie, wasn't able to come but we're so glad she allowed the kids to come with us. They are so special to us, and we are so excited to be here with them!" Grandma Em lovingly looked at Annmarie with a gentle smile.

Annmarie blushed and looked away but knew her Grandma was letting her know that all was forgiven. She stared intensely into her cup of tea, and thought, *Maybe I haven't screwed this up, yet.*

"Oh, I see. That's wonderful! Family is so important, isn't it? It's never too late! So, is Bonnie yer only child?"

"Well, Bonnie is Paul's mother. But we had another girl, our beloved Janet. She and her husband, Jacob, passed away in a car accident about twelve years ago. Annmarie lives with Bonnie and Paul, now." Grandma Em grabbed for a tissue as her eyes began to glisten. "I'm sorry, I don't talk about it much. Sometimes I just get a little choked up."

Annmarie looked over at her grandma and saw the pain in her face. Curious. She hadn't really ever given much thought to how hard it must have been for her grandparents to lose one of their daughters. She hadn't thought the conversation could get even more personal than nicknames!

"Oh, my goodness! I'm so sorry." Lily got up from the table and moved toward Em and hugged her as though they were lifelong friends. "I can't imagine losing a child."

Kennedy leaned over to whisper conspiratorially to Annmarie, "Mum is very affectionate. Get ready, she'll get to you next." Kennedy gave her a little wink.

Annmarie's heart started pounding faster. This only added to her discomfort. Annmarie buried her painful feelings for a reason, and again attempted to use her internal Whack-a-Mole mallet to force those rascally emotions deep down inside, where they belonged.

Just as Kennedy had warned, Lily came over to Annmarie and put her arms around her with a big motherly bear hug. Annmarie closed her eyes and focused on the cookies in her mouth and tried to ignore the uncomfortable affection.

"Sweet ladies. Ye are so blessed to have each other. Family is so important and special. We understand how ya feel. My husband, Colin passed away suddenly of a heart attack a few years back. I can't even begin to tell ya what a surprise it was for Cardy and me. My sweet parents surrounded us with love and help as I started my bakery. But, ya know, I do believe our loved ones are in heaven cheerin' us on here. I've even had dreams of seeing my sweet Colin.

Those dreams are gold to me. We once had a conversation in a dream. We were in this lovely garden, and he told me that heaven is like a window. They can see us and pray for us. Isn't that amazin'?" Lily dabbed at her own tears as she shared this revelation that obviously meant a lot to her.

Kennedy placed her hand on her mom's hand and looked lovingly at her. Annmarie wondered if it was true: if her mom and dad were watching and praying for her from heaven.

This thought reminded her of the cardinal symbolism she had read about, and her dreams. She remembered that cardinals were exceptional parents and even mated for life. Maybe they *were* watching her. Annmarie still wasn't sure, but the thought certainly brought her comfort.

"Oh my. I'm so sorry to get so emotional over this. Just like you said, it jus' hits ya from time to time," Lily said as she regained her composure with a sniff. "Well, how about you, Annmarie? Didn't ya say you were Cardy's age?"

Annmarie nodded yes, happy to change to a much safer subject.

"What do ya like to do? Any hobbies or interests?"

"I don't know," Annmarie answered sheepishly with a shrug. "I'm taking a photography class. I'm supposed to take pictures of Ireland for class, so I brought my camera along."

"Oh, that's wonderful. Ireland is beautiful, love! Cardy, maybe you could take Annmarie to some fun spots this week so she can get some good pictures. I'll happily give ya a few hours off."

"Sure, Mum. That sounds fun," Kennedy answered as she smiled at Annmarie. She literally had a twinkle in her eye. "I know a really beautiful place."

Annmarie took a third cookie and had some more tea. She shrugged her shoulders in response to the suggested outing. She was uncomfortable and eager to just be alone again. Kennedy was beautiful and altogether way out of her friendship league. She felt like a charity case, as though Kennedy was being forced to hang out with her, and she hated it.

"Okay, ladies. We should be getting back to our shop now," Lily said, looking at her wrist watch. She warmly invited them to come and chat anytime as they said their goodbyes and left.

"Well, that was fun wasn't it? I will have to get the recipe from Lily for those cookies. They were scrumptious, weren't they?" Grandma Em asked.

Annmarie had to agree. They *were* amazing.

Grandma Em invited Annmarie to check out some local stores in town with her. Annmarie was relieved that she had another chance. They browsed and walked and chatted about surface things. Annmarie sensed that Grandma Em knew she needed to tread lightly and go slowly with her. She felt even closer to her, even though they didn't talk about anything special. Just knowing how considerate Grandma Em was for her feelings made Annmarie trust her even more.

Later that day, Grandpa Eli and Paul returned from their fishing excursion. Paul burst through the front door and exclaimed that he was a born fisherman. He proudly displayed the prized cod that he caught. Grandma Em clapped with delight and told him how proud she was of him. Annmarie was pretty impressed too but played it cool.

"Are you going to use that as bait for Nessie, Paul?" Annmarie taunted.

"Very funny. Hey, just you wait, A! I'm going to find him." He winked.

"Our guide today was pretty impressed that Paul was so lucky. He gave me instructions on how to clean it so that we can fry it up and enjoy it for dinner."

"A, take a picture of me with your camera! I want to show Mom," Paul asked. "Your teacher might want to frame this one and put it in her classroom."

Annmarie laughed, but fetched her camera and took a slew of pictures of Paul and Grandpa Eli with the cod. "You are hilarious."

Grandpa went outside with the fish to clean it and Paul shared his fishing tales from the day. Apparently, he had a much larger fish on his hook, but it got away. He exaggerated that it had to have been at least 50 pounds. Paul also shared that he saw a fish that looked like an eel, convinced it had to be a relative of Nessie. Paul was epic comic relief.

Grandpa Eli suggested they refrigerate the fish for tomorrow and go to a classic Irish pub he'd heard about that served the best stew in town. They all agreed and made their way there. The atmosphere and food were excellent, and Grandpa Eli enjoyed a Guinness. Classic Irish music played in the background. Paul told everyone that they had just had a group of Irish dancers perform at his school for St. Patrick's Day. He told the waiter they should hire some of those Irish dancers in their curly wigs to dance at the pub.

The waiter nodded in agreement and winked at him. He told Paul that they did have dancers come from time to time for special events.

Annmarie had brought her camera along, hoping to catch some good pictures of the exciting hustle and bustle of the pub. She noticed that she didn't see anyone on their cell phones. Instead, people were laughing in conversation and enjoying connecting with one another around the tables. Since this was such an unusual, yet delightful, sight, Annmarie snuck in some candid shots in an attempt to capture the love and joy she was witnessing. Somehow, just watching all of these families and friends bonding brought happiness and peace to her heart.

After dinner, Annmarie went straight to her bedroom and flopped onto her bed. She didn't even have the energy to get into her pajamas or under the covers. She fell fast asleep and into another dream.

Chapter 11

Annmarie found herself back in the same cave, only this time it was darker and scarier. She looked at the ground and saw weeds growing up around her feet. The weeds continued to snake up her body at an alarming rate and within moments were wrapping around her waist.

She tried to pull her feet out of the patch of intimidating weeds, but it was as though they were stuck in concrete. She tried to cry out for help, but even though she felt air vibrate through her active vocal cords, no sound escaped her lips. Yet, she could hear the cardinal singing outside the cave. The weeds quickly tightened around her chest. Hardly able to breathe, she struggled, desperately fighting for her life.

Then she saw a glimmer of light come from the entrance of the cave, and she briefly saw the outline of a man before she had to look away because the light grew so bright.

Annmarie startled awake and shook her legs just to make sure she wasn't actually paralyzed. Her heart was pounding, and her palms were wet with sweat. Why did she keep dreaming about this cave? Why did she feel drawn to it and yet so afraid of it at the same time? She felt on the verge of another panic attack.

She tried to reassure herself that it had just been a dream, but she knew deep inside that it contained a message for her. She was more confused than ever and wondered if she should tell someone about the dreams.

Sunlight poured into her room from the window, the rays bathing her face in warmth and brightness, making her squint. *Well, I'm awake now!* She climbed out of her bed and went downstairs to join Grandma Em.

Annmarie could smell pancakes on the griddle, bacon sizzling and coffee brewing. The absence of the boys indicated that they were still asleep.

"Good morning, Annmarie!" Grandma cheerfully greeted. "I hope you are hungry; I'm making enough for an army!"

Annmarie was starving and everything smelled delicious. "Thank you."

Annmarie instinctively started to set the table for all four of them.

"Oh, thank you sweetie. Good idea. I'll cook, you set the table, and the boys can do the fun job of clean-up. That's teamwork!" Grandma smiled.

"Back home I usually do everything."

"Oh, really?"

"Well, yeah. Bonnie is always tired from work or not home and Paul usually has sports, so I just do it," Annmarie said.

"Annmarie, thank you for all the hard work you do for Bonnie and Paul at home."

Annmarie was puzzled. She didn't really understand why Grandma would thank her. In fact, she didn't think she had ever been thanked at all for helping out. She just felt like it was payment for letting her live with them.

"You are a very sweet young lady, Annmarie. I'm proud of you," Grandma Em said as she flipped the flapjacks.

Annmarie felt even more befuddled. What in the world had she ever done that would make anyone proud? *Grandma must be having an elderly moment. She's confused.* Annmarie shook her head and dismissed it, altogether.

"Kennedy is coming by to get you in about an hour to take you on a little hike. Her mom called me early this morning to let me know," Grandma Em said with a smile.

"Okay," Annmarie said as she placed the butter and syrup on the table. She wasn't interested in going anywhere with Kennedy, but it sounded like she'd have to make the best of it. She *had* said she knew a cool place for pictures.

Annmarie heard Grandpa Eli laugh loudly, and he and Paul racing down the stairs sounded like a stampede! Grandpa kicked it into high gear, acting like he was Paul's age.

"Be careful!" Grandma Em scolded Grandpa Eli. She worried about the boys going too far, but she loved their playful interaction and could see it was good for her husband.

The four of them sat down together and enjoyed their pancakes. Grandma Em informed Grandpa and Paul that they were the clean-up crew. With some good-natured whining, the boys complied and started bussing the table.

Not long after breakfast, there was a knock at the door. Grandma Em insisted Annmarie answer it, as she was showing the boys how to use the dishwasher.

Annmarie opened the door and found Kennedy, as she had expected, with a big smile on her freckled face. Annmarie welcomed her inside.

"Hello!" Grandma and Grandpa greeted Kennedy, but Paul's jaw had dropped, and he was dumbstruck. Annmarie stifled a giggle as she could see that Paul was in love at first sight.

Kennedy's curly, bright red hair was pulled back into a loose ponytail. A brilliant blue plaid flannel shirt intensified her jeweled blue eyes. She just had a glow to her that shined brightly from the inside out. Annmarie introduced Kennedy to Paul and her Grandpa Eli, and she shook their hands.

"I'll be back in a minute, Kennedy. I'm gonna get my camera." Annmarie ran up to her room and grabbed her camera and a sweatshirt to tie around her waist in case she got cold. When she came back downstairs, she noticed that Paul had moved curiously close to Kennedy and was trying to impress her with his basketball knowledge.

"Paul, we're going for a walk. Kennedy is going to show me some places to take pictures for school. Do you want to come along?" Annmarie asked.

Paul frowned as he faced a difficult choice. "Grandpa and I are fishing again, but can I come with you another time, Kennedy?" It was so obvious that he was captivated by her. Kennedy nodded her head and smiled.

Annmarie and Kennedy quickly exited the house. "I'm so sorry about Paul. He's extra," Annmarie apologized.

"Nah, he's okay," Kennedy said. "Well, follow me. Are you ready to see the beauty of Ireland?"

"Sure. Let's go."

Kennedy led the way to a park with rolling hills and green, lush grass. Off in the distance she could see a castle-like structure. Someone who knew Kennedy waved at her and called out, "Hey, Cardy!" Kennedy waved in reply.

"How did you get that nickname?"

"Yeah, it's an interestin' story. Back when I was tiny, we flew to the US to meet some friends of the family. I was in the backyard and there was this bird called a cardinal that perched on my head. Cardinals are red and when I was a baby, my hair color was almost a match for the cardinal's feathers. It only stayed briefly but long enough for my mum to get a photo! Everyone there saw it and teased that I must be like Saint Francis of Assisi. My mum started callin' me Cardy, which is short for Cardinal. I know it's strange, but it just stuck and now all my family an' friends call me Cardy. That baby picture of me still hangs in our house. It's so embarrassing."

Annmarie was shocked.

"Annmarie, are you okay? Ya look a bit flushed!"

"No, no. I'm fine. I just…I love cardinals. I actually saw one outside my window."

Kennedy glanced at her, curiously. "Are ya sure? Cause, cardinals don't live in Ireland. I wish they did, cause they're beautiful."

"Oh…I must have been mistaken." Annmarie was dumbfounded. She *knew* that she had seen a cardinal outside of her window after pleading for God to help her! She'd been dreaming about a cardinal for weeks, and now, she's met someone who was named after a cardinal? *How bizarre!* she thought to herself.

The girls walked up and down hills, enjoying the scenery of various trees and flowers, until they reached the top of a very large hill that looked out over the town and ocean. Annmarie was breathing heavily because she wasn't used to hiking and climbing hills. It was a magnificent view. A refreshing wind was whipping, and Annmarie was so glad because she was hot and tired.

"Here's a great place for some pictures, Annmarie," Kennedy said. She found a patch of grass, plopped down in it, closed her eyes and sighed deeply. "I love just laying down right here. This is where I come to unwind."

Annmarie was in awe of the beauty of the landscape. She took many pictures and even snapped some shots of Kennedy in the grass.

"Okay, now I'm gonna show ya a secret place. I brought a picnic lunch for us and we can chill out and eat there. It'll be fantastic. It's just beyond these trees. My friends and I like to hang out there. There's even a really cool hidden cave there," Kennedy offered.

Annmarie's tummy butterflies flew into a frenzy. *Wait just a minute! A cardinal is leading me to a secret cave? This is just too weird!* She pinched herself to make sure she wasn't dreaming again.

As they continued to walk, Annmarie could see the cave, hidden in the side of the next hill. As soon as they stepped foot inside, Annmarie's skin tingled into giant goosebumps. She had seen this place before.

Kennedy led her to a boulder near the entrance, and she sat down in the exact way she remembered in her dreams. Annmarie was speechless. Something supernatural was going on, but she couldn't quite understand it. It was too personal, precious and weighty.

They continued to explore the cave for a few minutes, and Annmarie's awe continued to grow. Everything was exactly the same! Not only the boulder, but Kennedy pointed out carvings on the walls that were identical to the ones she had seen before: the birds, the Celtic cross, and even the door.

Hesitantly, Annmarie asked about the door. "Um...why would someone carve the shape of a door into a cave wall? I mean...It doesn't open, so what's the point?"

"Well, do you see these carvings around the door itself?" Annmarie nodded.

"It's said that it means, 'The door opens for one who chooses.' But others will say that the more accurate translation is, 'The door opens for one who unlocks their heart.'"

See what I want to show you. Unlock your heart and walk through the door. The voice from Annmarie's dream echoed in her mind.

"But how?" Annmarie slapped her hand against the rock in frustration. "How are we supposed to walk through something made of stone?"

Kennedy smiled, "Perhaps there's more than one way? We all have to figure that out on our own, wouldn't you say?"

Her eyes seemed to twinkle with some sort of shared secret. Unfortunately, Annmarie didn't know what the secret was!

"Isn't it just glorious, Annmarie? I've shared it with you now, so you can call it your secret cave, too." Kennedy smiled wide.

Although Annmarie was more confused than ever, Kennedy's enthusiasm was infectious, and she couldn't help but return her smile.

After they explored the cave for a few more minutes, they walked back outside where Kennedy unpacked the yellow and white checkered tablecloth and picnic goods she had prepared. They sat down on the blanket as sunshine bathed the entire area.

The girls enjoyed homemade peanut butter and jam sandwiches, cheeses and more shortbreads. Annmarie was happily surprised at how at ease she felt being there with Kennedy yet was still intimidated by her beauty and charm. Kennedy seemed to be authentic, but she never knew for sure. Annmarie had been wrong before.

Kennedy explained that she worked very hard to help her mom with the shop, which cut into her social time, but she didn't mind. She still found time to hang out with friends here and there. She shared how boys were really awkward around her just the same way Paul was. She confessed that many girls at school were mean to her because of it. Annmarie was stunned that someone like her could relate to rejection.

"Well, I bet if you lived where I lived, you would be treated like a queen by everyone," Annmarie said.

"I don't want to be treated like a queen, Annmarie. I just want to have true friends who like me for who I am. People who will just be who they really are and let me be who I really am."

Annmarie felt badly for judging Kennedy. Could it really be that other kids—even really brilliant, beautiful kids—had issues with fitting in?

The girls packed up the tablecloth and picnic food and headed back home, although Annmarie didn't want to leave. She felt almost an urgency to return to this new secret place. She asked Kennedy if it would be safe for her to come back on her own the next day.

Kennedy looked at Annmarie with a twinkle in her eye, as though she had a secret to tell.

"Yes, of course," she said. The sun hit her red hair in such a way that she dazzled like a ruby.

Kennedy brought Annmarie back to the cottage, and when they entered the door, Paul dashed downstairs to welcome them. He told them all about how he caught another big fish and how he was sure that he spotted Nessie this time.

He awkwardly stared at Kennedy, hoping his story would impress her. Kennedy sweetly nodded and smiled kindly at him. At one point she gave a little wink to Annmarie who tried to stifle her laughter.

Kennedy gently took Annmarie by the hand and gave her a gentle squeeze as she said goodbye. Annmarie felt a connection with her she never would have expected.

After answering questions about her day and sharing a bit of her adventure with her grandparents and Paul, Annmarie flew to her bedroom and furiously wrote a journal entry about what had happened.

She laughed at the idea that Kennedy was her Ruby! Awe and wonder filled her heart as she pondered the events of the day and how they correlated to the string of dreams she had been having over the past few months. She could hardly wait to go back to the cave.

However, in the next moment, fear attacked Annmarie as she contemplated all that could go wrong on her own. What if she were kidnapped or injured—or worse yet, killed? She was in a foreign country. What if Kennedy was really setting her up for something terrible?

Yet, the fear of *not* investigating the cave more thoroughly far outweighed any other fears. She disregarded them and settled her resolve: *I'm going back!*

Chapter 12

Early the next morning, Grandma asked Annmarie what she would like to do for the day. She offered to take her into town to shop again or to go on a boat ride if she wanted. She declined the offer and shared how Kennedy had taken her to a special place and she wanted to take a hike there again, by herself. Grandma Em nixed her request to go alone, but offered to accompany her.

"Grandma Em, I really want to go by myself, just for a little bit. I promise I will have my phone and I will call you when I get there, and I promise I'll be safe," Annmarie begged.

Grandma Em was not okay with this decision, but she also knew that Annmarie was responsible and wanted to connect with her. So, she finally caved in and gave her permission. She told Annmarie to call her every half-hour and that she couldn't be gone for longer than two hours.

Annmarie agreed to the conditions and got ready for her hike. Grandma Em packed some fruit and cookies for her to snack on. She also made sure Annmarie's cell phone was charged up to 100%. Grandma Em wasn't at ease with Annmarie going off by herself, but she realized it was very important to her.

"I'd like you to be home no later than noon."

"Okay, I won't be long. I know exactly where I'm going. Kennedy showed me the way," Annmarie assured her.

As she walked, Annmarie carefully watched for all the landmarks that led her to the secret cave. She climbed up the rolling hills and found the big hill where the cave was located. Again, she was hot and sweaty, plus sore from the previous climb. She was breathing heavily, and her heart was racing in excitement about exploring the area. She got to the top of the hill and laid down right where Kennedy had the day before.

She relaxed there a few minutes with her eyes closed. She consciously breathed in the fresh, crisp air and let her body recover from the climb. She then sat up and scanned the area to make sure she was alone. She didn't see anyone, so she stood up and started walking toward the secret cave.

When she arrived, Annmarie walked in and placed her hand on the icy cold cave wall. Sitting down on the boulder, she looked around again. There was a damp smell in the air that oddly didn't bother her. As her eyes adjusted to the darkness of the cave, she examined a multitude of names carved in the interior wall. She saw Sally, John, Patrick, Mary and toward the bottom even Kennedy!

She walked further into the cave, closer to the wall where the doorway was carved. She felt her foot kick something. She assumed it was a rock as there were quite a few on the ground but when she looked more closely, she saw that it wasn't a rock at all.

It was a very strange, old-fashioned looking pair of glasses. They were silver wire-rimmed, and the lenses were a light pink color. She wondered if Kennedy or one of her friends had accidentally forgotten them there. She grabbed her phone to text Kennedy but hesitated. Why not try them on, first?

The moment she looked through the lenses, her eyes were flooded by a bright light! Annmarie panicked and frantically tore the glasses from her eyes.

Instantly, the cave was dark again.

"What the heck?" She yelled as she dropped the glasses on the ground where she had found them and sped out of the cave. Safely outside again, she breathed deeply, waiting for her frantically racing heart to slow. Perplexed, she debated whether she should leave or stay. At first, she wondered if those were special virtual reality glasses or something.

She thought about texting Kennedy a picture of the glasses to ask her about them. Were they magical or was she hallucinating after the long hike back up the hills? After looking around again to see if anyone else was nearby, she decided to sit down for a snack and think about what to do.

About half-an-hour had passed and Annmarie decided it best to call Grandma Em to let her know she was okay. After assuring her that all was well, she marched herself back into the cave to examine the peculiar spectacles. She picked them up again and looked closely at the silver-wire rims. As she examined them, she touched the lenses and shook them as though something would shake out of them. They were pretty normal looking. Nothing spectacular. No secret wires or anything.

Finally, she gathered up enough courage to put them on again. Just like before, her eyes were flooded with light.

Chapter 13

It took a few moments for Annmarie's eyes to adjust to the light. The cave had lit up as though it were noonday, and she could see every pebble and carving clearly. Then Annmarie saw the source of the light—blazing through the edges of the door carving, the rays illuminated the entire cave.

She slowly approached the door. Whereas the door had definitely been a carving of cold rock when she had pounded on it before, as she lay her hand on it, she could feel warmth seeping through from the other side.

The other side? Annmarie, you have lost your mind! There is no other side—it's stone! Annmarie slid the glasses down to the tip of her nose and looked over them at what again appeared to be a plain carved outline of a door on a cold cave wall.

See what I want to show you. Unlock your heart and walk through the door."

The voice seemed to vibrate through her entire body, and although she felt completely crazy, it was almost as if it came from the other side of the door! *Okay, how am I supposed to open a stone door?*

Annmarie examined the door again, top to bottom. There was no sign of a doorknob, so how was she supposed to open it? Her eyes settled on the flowers carved on the door, where a doorknocker might hang in the center. She reached up her hand and began to trace the carving with her index finger.

Suddenly, the flowers began a pulsating glow and she felt the door shudder at her touch! *Could it be that simple?* Annmarie gently placed her entire left palm over the flowers. The light under her hand intensified and the door began to swing open! Without lifting her hand away from the door, she pushed gently, and it continued to swing open in front of her.

As the door opened, the light became so bright, she covered her face with her right arm. Looking down at her feet, she saw the cold dirt floor of the cave transition into bright green grass on the other side of the threshold. Slowly she lowered her arm as her eyes adjusted to the brightness.

Annmarie felt like she had landed square in the middle of Oz, like Dorothy. She stood still and just examined the scenery. All the colors she saw were more vibrant than she had ever seen before. It was as if everything was somehow lit up and magnified. In the distance, she saw a waterfall flowing down the side of a cliff, a rainbow glistening in the mist. It was perfect!

She stepped into the grass, leaving the damp cave behind. The warmth of the sun infused her skin and she could hear the roar of the waterfall. How could mere glasses supply all of this? She stood in the scene as though she had stepped into a masterpiece painting in a museum.

She grabbed the glasses again and slowly pushed them up toward her forehead so that she could peek and see what everything looked like without them. The light disappeared, and in its place was the darkness of cave walls. It was as though with the glasses on she was travelling, yet without them returned to the place she started! The strange thing was that not only was the gorgeous scene gone, but so were the sounds and the feeling of sunshine warming her skin.

She methodically slipped the glasses back down over her eyes and was again in paradise. She looked down at her feet and she could see the grass and flowers and could hear a faint humming sound.

All of her senses seemed more sensitive. She bent down to look more closely, and she could hear the sound of singing in the grass. It was as though each blade of grass was alive and celebrating with a song. The song started tickling her toes and Annmarie felt overwhelmed by the sensation.

She then noticed that she was near a pathway. She followed it to a beautifully manicured flower garden. A familiar floral scent gently caressed her nose. She recognized it as the smell that flowed through her dream! Annmarie saw other people walking around enjoying themselves in the gardens. Some were walking hand-in-hand while others were alone, just resting and relaxing. Annmarie wondered if they could see her. Even her eyesight had intensified, and she could see for miles.

Am I going crazy?

A kind and quiet voice from behind responded audibly to her silent thought, "You aren't crazy, Annmarie."

Surprised, Annmarie spun around to see who was there and found herself face-to-face with a man. He had brown, wavy hair and deep blue, mesmerizing eyes like tractor beams drawing her in. His kindness caught Annmarie off-guard. She knew she should be wary of strangers, but she felt like she knew him. Somehow, she was sure that he was safe.

The man started to chuckle. He put his hand out to shake hers. Annmarie reflexively grasped his hand in return.

"How did you know what I was thinking?" she asked.

"My name is Mr. Immanuel. I'm the gardener here. I saw you pop in and wanted to warmly welcome you, Annmarie."

She was bewildered that he not only had known what she was thinking but knew her name as well. Just then she decided to test him. She thought, *What is your favorite color, Mr. Immanuel?*

He grinned at her, his eyes twinkling with amusement.

"I know *your* favorite color is red," He answered.

Annmarie's eyes widened with shock. Ever since she had seen the cardinal in her dreams, she had been deeply drawn to the color red. Suddenly, she panicked, feeling exposed and afraid. Annmarie wanted to hide. This man knew way too much about her.

"Don't be afraid, Annmarie. I am your friend."

This time, Annmarie heard his voice, but he hadn't moved his mouth. She was tempted to remove the glasses and be done with this strange, uncomfortable adventure.

"Annmarie, would you like to take a walk with me? I'd like to show you around. I promise I will not see into your thoughts anymore," Mr. Immanuel promised with a grin.

Annmarie agreed to go with him even though it was completely against her nature. In real life, she would never ever walk or talk with a stranger, but she felt compelled to walk with him. She wondered if she would bump into the cave wall or something, but she never did. She thought she must be dreaming. There was something about Mr. Immanuel that felt comfortable and she was intrigued by all that was transpiring in this secret paradise.

He took her by the hand, and they walked through the garden. There were hundreds of beds of roses and each bed had their own unique color, scent and atmosphere. When they approached a bed of red roses, Mr. Immanuel picked one that was in full bloom and handed it to Annmarie.

"This is called a 'Freedom Rose.' You are like this rose, Annmarie."

Annmarie received the flower and its thick aroma surrounded her like a silk blanket. She breathed it in and began to tear up. As the smell overpowered her senses, she felt something snap in her heart. Tears rolled down her cheeks, and she was confused about why she was crying.

"You are beautiful, my dear," Mr. Immanuel encouraged her. He gave her a linen handkerchief to wipe her eyes and waited patiently for her to be ready to go on.

As he spoke to her, the tears came faster, and she began to sob. The words he spoke were breaking through her walls and touching a deep place in her heart. She had never *felt* beautiful, but this man seemed so incredibly authentic and sure of what he was saying to her. His opinion, although she had just met him, seemed to carry weight. It was as if he had found the soft spot in her shell.

"Come with me, sweet one. There's more to see." He held out his hand for her.

He showed her the lilies, carnations, petunias and lavender. Annmarie especially liked the lavender. She loved the smell because it had a soothing effect on her. They stopped and lingered a while. All of the floral scents had been kicked up a notch in this place. Compared to home, everything was more vivid.

"Would you like to rest here a bit?" Mr. Immanuel asked.

Annmarie nodded her head. Mr. Immanuel snapped his fingers and two Adirondack chairs appeared. They sat down and inhaled the soothing lavender together.

"We put the lavender here to help people relax on their journey through the garden," Mr. Immanuel shared. He then tied her Freedom Rose into a small bundle that she could carry.

"Where am I?" Annmarie asked Mr. Immanuel.

"You're in my garden."

"I mean, I just was in Ireland and then I found this cave, and these glasses I'm wearing brought me here. Am I still on the earth? Where am I, exactly?" Annmarie asked.

Mr. Immanuel smiled gleefully again. "I know all about your story. This is our secret place, Annmarie. We have been preparing you for this meeting all your life. If I told you where you were right now, you wouldn't believe me. Just trust me when I say this is a good land. In time, you will understand. We are so happy you are here now. Your timing is perfect."

Just then a majestic, larger-than-life monarch butterfly soared over and landed on Annmarie's head. She was delighted and kept as still as she could. She raised her finger up to it, hoping it would walk onto it, which it did. Then she gingerly placed the butterfly onto the Freedom Rose she had been carrying in her other hand.

"I think it likes me!" she exclaimed.

Mr. Immanuel smiled. "Shall we move on?"

"Yes!"

They walked along and found a flower bed that was off the main garden path. It had some wilting daisies and sunflowers, surrounded by raggedy weeds.

"These flowers need full sun, but they are being overshadowed by these large thorny bushes and shrubs," Mr. Immanuel explained.

"Oh my! This isn't right. Will these flowers die here?" Annmarie asked with concern.

Mr. Immanuel looked at Annmarie with compassion in his eyes. "You're right, Annmarie. This patch was planted on the outskirts of the garden, but it should be inside. These flowers need to be cared for. They need to be nurtured back to health. Would you like to help me transplant this bed into a new place? I have the perfect spot. I'd like to place it smack dab in the center of the garden where it will thrive."

"YES!" Annmarie said excitedly. She was passionate about helping these flowers. She strangely could identify with this off-kilter garden that was wilted, uncared for and outcast.

Mr. Immanuel nodded in agreement and handed her a

spade and some plastic cups. They first filled the plastic cups half-way with fresh soil and carefully scooped up the dying daisies and sunflowers and placed them in the cups, then secured them with more soil.

They were preparing to return to the garden when Mr. Immanuel suggested they tear out the weeds and sprinkle the area with grass seed. Annmarie eagerly placed the cups nearby and helped pull out the weeds. They were really tough to get out for her, but they came out extremely easily for Mr. Immanuel. Seeing the struggle Annmarie was having with this, he gave her a special tool to make it easier. In no time, they had pulled the weeds, tilled the soil and spread the grass seed. Mr. Immanuel blessed the area and sprinkled it with water.

"Okay, Annmarie. We're ready to replant. Follow me, my dear."

They walked through patches of all kinds of tropical flowers, succulents and wildflowers. Every kind of flower imaginable seemed to have a place in this massive, beautiful garden. Finally, they reached a small patch of dirt. It was as though it had been waiting for them.

"Okay, Annmarie. Here's the perfect spot. There's adequate sunshine, rain and honey bees in this area to help these flowers. This is dark, rich soil. The plants will thrive here."

Annmarie nodded her head in agreement. She had never really planted anything before, so this was all new to her. Just a few feet away, she saw someone who looked like Jonathan from school in another patch of the garden.

As she looked his way it was as if the glasses magnified her vision and zoomed in on his face. It *was* him! Annmarie couldn't believe it! How in the world could it be that she and Jonathan could both be here when she was in Ireland and he was still at home—an ocean away? It was crazy!

"Excuse me, Mr. Immanuel. I see someone from my school over there. How can this be?"

Mr. Immanuel, busy in the dirt, looked up at Annmarie and smiled again.

"There are many who know about the garden, Annmarie. People you know and people you've not yet met. Jonathan often comes here to visit."

Annmarie quickly bent down to help Mr. Immanuel in the soil, hiding from Jonathan. She was really confused.

"Do you want to visit with him, Annmarie?" He asked.

Annmarie's eyes widened and she stared into Mr. Immanuel's face like a deer frozen in the headlights of an oncoming car.

"He won't bite you. I promise," He teased.

"I can't!" She blurted out.

Just then, she looked back over her shoulder at Jonathan again and their eyes met. He smiled and nodded in her direction as if he was acknowledging her and then he moved on to continue what he was doing.

"Mr. Immanuel. How is it that I could see Jonathan's face so close? Are these glasses like magnifying glasses? Jonathan just smiled at me. He saw me!"

Mr. Immanuel laughed again. He was a very joyful fellow. "Annmarie, when you are here, your vision is magnified, and you can see more clearly. Your desire to see Jonathan's face empowered you to zoom in."

"Wow. Yes, it's true! I feel like everything is just brighter and more alive here. It's amazing!" Annmarie gushed. "Am I dreaming this or what?"

Mr. Immanuel continued to laugh. "Okay, sweet pea. The fresh new soil is ready. It's time to plant these golden gems."

When Annmarie turned to get the flowers, rather than browning petals, she saw exactly what Mr. Immanuel had described—literal golden gemstones in the dirt cups! She looked at him quizzically.

"These are the life-seeds of the sunflowers and daisies we are planting here." Mr. Immanuel said. Annmarie was stunned at their transformation. She saw him planting the new gem-seeds in the soil, and as she planted her own gems, she noticed there were golden flecks in the rich ground that sparkled in the sunshine. It was stunning.

"Will the seeds grow, Mr. Immanuel?"

"Yes. They will be a beautiful addition to my garden. Gold is a very precious color to me," Mr. Immanuel shared.

They continued planting all the gem-seeds, and as soon as they were finished, a small cloud came over and proceeded to rain on the flower bed they had just planted together.

Annmarie was bursting with happiness and anticipation for the new patch of garden. She looked up to see Mr. Immanuel's face beaming at her with an intense love she had never felt before. He stretched his arm out to hold her hand and Annmarie shocked herself by throwing her arms around his waist in the biggest bear hug she had ever given.

As she nuzzled into his shoulder, monster-sized chills welled up from inside of her and, strangely, she began to tremble. Earlier, when he had given her the Freedom Rose, she had felt a small degree of this, but now it was as though a dam had broken open in her heart. She felt physically weak and wobbly as her legs turned to spaghetti and she began to fall but Mr. Immanuel held her in his arms and whispered tenderly, like a father to his child.

"You are precious, sweet one. Everything is going to be okay, my ray of sunshine. We will watch this garden grow and bloom together. It's our special garden."

This river of love he unleashed overpowered her and she was lost in it. Never before had she felt such safety and connectedness to someone. She came alive in his embrace, crying and laughing all at the same time as anxiety washed right out of her heart.

"Have I discovered heaven? I never want to go home!" Annmarie exclaimed.

Mr. Immanuel hugged Annmarie tightly and kissed her forehead. "You belong here, Annmarie. You are always here," He assured her.

She had no idea what that meant but it didn't matter. She was here now and overjoyed at this unbelievable discovery. Resting in his arms was like being wrapped up in a warm blanket, sipping hot buttered punch on a wintry night. Just then, a bright-red sparkling cardinal flew overhead, and Annmarie burst into laughter. "I'm pretty sure cardinals don't fly in Ireland. Cardy told me."

"You're not in Ireland, my dear," Mr. Immanuel answered. "You've had a long journey today, Annmarie. Let's rest on this picnic blanket." She looked over her right shoulder where he was pointing and saw a magnificent red and white picnic blanket, set up with a variety of fruits, bread and refreshments.

With a smile, Mr. Immanuel handed Annmarie some strawberries. They were the most beautiful strawberries she'd ever seen, perfectly shaped and a deep, beautiful shade of red. She took one bite and was amazed at how delicious it was. The taste was as vivid as the colors. "Wow, that's amazing!"

"I honestly feel like I'm dreaming. I'm waiting for Paul to wake me up from this dream, like he usually does," Annmarie's wry grin quickly morphed into an expression of near horror.

"Oh, my goodness! I just realized I'm supposed to be calling my Grandma!" She reached up to touch her glasses to make sure they were still on her head. A slight panic rose up from her belly as she wondered how long she had been gone. It felt like she had been there for many hours.

"Don't worry about the time, Annmarie. You will be back in Ireland right on time," Mr. Immanuel assured her.

Mr. Immanuel's face brought her whole being a peace she had never known existed. She decided to stop worrying and just enjoy another delicious strawberry. She felt perfectly safe and happy.

Suddenly, a little, black, curly-haired dog scampered over to greet them. He was so excited to see her and licked her cheek. She had always loved dogs and just had a feeling Mr. Immanuel knew that, too. She fell backwards and let him lick and tickle her face. The dog licked her so hard her glasses went flying, the weight of the sweet dog vanishing along with the light, and she immediately found herself lying on the cold dirt of the cave.

She rubbed her eyes, adjusting to the darkness. She frantically groped around for the magic glasses, but they had disappeared. The carving on the door had faded back to cold, lifeless stone. Slamming her hand against the flowers, she cried, "Open up! I want to go back! Open!" Yet, no matter what she tried, the door remained dark.

Unable to find them inside, Annmarie ran outside of the cave to search for the spectacles. After a solid thirty minutes of scouring the area with no luck, Annmarie sat down and cried hopelessly. She *had* to find a way to go back. She spotted her phone to check the time and was dumbfounded to discover she had only been gone a total of 35 minutes of Ireland time.

That's impossible! My phone must've broken or something. But then she remembered Mr. Immanuel had said she would be back in time. Her mind raced, trying to recall the events in the secret place. It was completely unexplainable.

Giving up on the glasses, knowing her grandmother would be expecting her, Annmarie decided to run back to the house right away to journal her extraordinary experience. She thought about reaching out to Kennedy to process it. She couldn't tell Paul or her grandparents because they might think she was crazy. She wondered if she really *was* crazy.

When she finally returned, breathless as she was not a runner, Grandma Em smiled inquisitively and asked why she was back so early.

She couldn't catch her breath to answer right away.

"Good heavens, sweetie! Are you having a panic attack? What happened out there? Did you get scared?" Grandma Em rushed at Annmarie to adequately assess the situation.

"I'm fine...Grandma. No, I was...just running," Annmarie assured her between breaths and laughter.

She ran straight up to her room, grabbed her bird journal, and flopped on the bed, taking some deep breaths to regain her composure. She wrote down everything she could remember about her encounter in the garden.

As she was recording the events, many of the sensations she had experienced remained with her. It was as though her very cellular structure had absorbed each one. The deep, delicious peace and perfect love she had felt in Mr. Immanuel's embrace was still fully with her. She heard the familiar voice gently whisper, "Happy sweet 16, precious one!" She had completely forgotten! A cleansing, joy-filled tear trickled down her cheek. This was the most beautiful and profound birthday of her life.

However, she was still upset about losing the glasses and hoped that they were still around somewhere. She started to hatch a plan to return to really scour the cave again. Mentally exhausted, she laid her journal down, flopped back on the bed and closed her eyes. She grabbed her pillow and held it close, pretending it was the cutest dog she had ever seen and she fell into a deep, restful sleep.

Chapter 14

Grandma Em, Grandpa Eli, Paul and Annmarie were feeling sad that it was their last day in Ireland. Annmarie was determined to go back to the cave one more time to search for the glasses again. She didn't know how to make it happen because they had plans to go for a boat cruise.

Annmarie asked Grandma Em if she could just stay behind but was denied. Grandma Em didn't feel good about that at all. Annmarie decided that if worse came to worse, she would just sneak out of the house with a flashlight while everyone was sleeping.

They all got dressed up and walked into town to eat at the local pub that touted the greatest sandwiches in all of Ireland. They walked past Lily and Kennedy's bakery to say goodbye and thank you.

Grandma Em asked Lily if there was a way to have her delicious shortbreads shipped to the US. Lily blushed and said that people often made that request. She handed

Grandma Em a business card and told her that she would do her best to send them whenever she would order. Grandma Em was thrilled.

Paul asked Kennedy if he could have her phone number so he could text her. Kennedy smiled warmly, took his phone and entered her number. Kennedy then moved from behind the counter to where Annmarie was standing. Annmarie had been looking down at the ground the whole time because she hated to say goodbye.

"Annmarie. I'll miss ya. Keep in touch?"

Annmarie looked up and saw Kennedy smiling at her with the same warmth she had felt when Mr. Immanuel looked at her. She reached out for a hug, and they gave each other a solid squeeze.

"You've seen it," Kennedy whispered. "I'll see you there."

Annmarie's jaw dropped open as she pulled away in shock.

Kennedy let out an amused chuckle and threw Annmarie a wink as she went to attend some other customers while Grandma Em and Lily chatted.

Annmarie wanted to chase Kennedy down, but Grandpa Eli reminded them they had a reservation at the restaurant, so she was dragged away. Annmarie kicked herself for not discussing her adventure with Kennedy sooner!

The family browsed around the area again just soaking in the atmosphere, and Annmarie took some fun pictures. Paul connected with Grandpa Eli in shared goofiness. They were like two little boys laughing and teasing one another. Annmarie could see that Paul clearly had gotten his sense of humor from Grandpa.

Grandma Em took Annmarie into a little shop with some cute clothes. It had been a long time since she had shopped for clothing, so Annmarie was a bit apprehensive about trying anything on.

Grandma enthusiastically pulled clothing off the racks, draping an ever-increasing pile over Annmarie's arm. Disregarding her apprehension, she decided to humor her grandmother and began to try on the outfits Em had selected.

Used to baggy, oversized sweatshirts and jeans, Annmarie felt out of her element as she tried on sundresses, slacks that clung to her hips and shirts that actually revealed her shape.

A particular ruby-red top caught her attention. Grandma nodded her approval and handed her a pair of black skinny capris and espadrille sandals to complete the look.

As Annmarie perused her reflection, she brushed her hair away from her face, tucking it behind her ears. Gazing at herself up and down, she saw something she'd never seen before—a pretty girl.

Is that me? It wasn't just that she could see a figure that wasn't hidden behind a mask of baggy clothing. As she looked into her own eyes—something she didn't think she'd ever really done—she saw peace, confidence, and joy radiating from behind them.

"Oh, Annie, you look beautiful! We're getting those!" Grandma Em gathered up quite a few other items she liked as well and, as Annmarie got changed into her old outfit, took them to the counter to pay for them.

Annmarie walked out and her eyes widened at the sight of her grandmother holding one bag with shirts and pants, and another with three pairs of shoes.

"Grandma! You didn't have to get all of that!"

"Oh, don't be silly, dear! Now you'll be all set to go back to school. These all looked lovely on you! I simply couldn't resist. What are grandmothers for, if not to spoil their granddaughters?"

Annmarie took the bags out of Grandma Em's hands and gave her a grateful hug. "Thank you, Grandma," she whispered.

"You're more than welcome, sweetheart," she whispered in response.

"Now! Let's go find where those boys wandered off to!"

That night, after everyone was in bed, Annmarie decided she had to sneak out of the house to go to the cave one more time. She just couldn't get it out of her mind. She felt as though she would die if she couldn't go back to the garden!

She found a flashlight in the kitchen drawer and a drawstring bag that she would use to contain the glasses if she found them. She absolutely *had* to see Mr. Immanuel and their special garden one more time. She promised herself that if she had another chance to go, she would boldly approach Jonathan, too. She was a girl on a mission.

She went through the back door as quietly as she could, but it was no use. Paul spotted her. She was caught red-handed.

"Where are you going, A?" Paul whispered.

"What are you doing up? Why aren't you sleeping? It's late!"

"I don't know. I can't sleep. I came down to get a glass of water."

"Well, go back upstairs now, and go to sleep," Annmarie commanded.

Paul laughed sarcastically at her, "Yeah, right! Where are you going? You weren't trying to run away, were you?" Paul asked.

Annmarie was beyond frustrated. However, she suddenly had an idea to invite him along to help her find the glasses. It seemed like that was her best bet.

"Well, okay Paul. You got me. I was going to this cave that Kennedy showed me earlier this week. There was a pair of glasses someone left there, and I thought I would get them to give to Kennedy because they might be hers. If you help me find them, I will buy you a candy bar at the airport. But you have to keep this a secret."

Paul nodded his head. Food had always been a good bargaining tool for Paul. "Okay! Let's go. Cool. Do you think she'll be there? Should I text her to see if she wants to meet us there? Maybe she's awake too!"

"Absolutely NOT! I told you this was a secret! That means you can't tell anyone!"

Paul wrinkled his nose in confusion, but he agreed to go along with her plan.

Annmarie was actually kind of glad he was with her. She was a little nervous about going by herself in the dark. Who knew what kind of animals or people would be around at that time of night?

"So, what do the glasses look like?" Paul asked as he rummaged through the drawer for another flashlight.

"Okay, they are kind of old-fashioned looking. They have a silver frame and the lenses are kind of pinkish. They aren't anything special." She didn't want him to know how special they really were because he might put them on or do something stupid.

"If they aren't special then why would you go to so much trouble to get them late at night, A?" Paul asked suspiciously.

"I was just up for a nighttime adventure is all. I remembered seeing them and I wanted to do something nice for Kennedy," Annmarie shrugged.

"Okay, whatever you say!"

"Please be super quiet though, Paul. We don't want to wake up Grandma and Grandpa," Annmarie commanded.

Paul shook his head. "Duh."

Finally, the two went off into the dark night. It was much colder outside. They both could see their breath as they hiked up the hills to the cave. As they walked, Paul's excitement to be along on the adventure was obvious as he chatted along the way. Annmarie just smiled and listened patiently, responding every so often so he knew she was paying attention. *He really is a sweet kid*, Annmarie thought with affection.

They finally reached the cave and started searching.

"WOW! Is this a real cave?"

"SHHHHHHH!" Annmarie tried to silence him. "Yes, Paul. It is a real cave. Kennedy showed it to me a few days ago. Now let's look for those glasses and be so careful. Point your flashlight at the ground so you don't step on them," Annmarie instructed.

"WHAT?!" Paul ran inside the cave and inspected every nook and cranny. He was exploding with excitement as he saw the names and pictures carved on the inside wall. "AWESOME!" he shouted as if he had found pirate booty.

Annmarie was now second-guessing herself for letting Paul come. She was worried he might carelessly step on the precious glasses.

"Okay, Paul. Yes, it's cool but could you please help me look for those glasses, and please, please, *please* don't step on them!" Annmarie begged. "You look inside the cave and I'll look outside here."

Annmarie carefully examined the perimeter of the cave and the surrounding grass again, hoping they would just pop up somewhere. She pointed her flashlight up into the trees to see if she saw them dangling from a branch or something.

"Any luck, Paul?" Annmarie asked.

"Hey, did you see this cool cross thing?" Paul asked in response. "I saw these in the stores in town."

"That's called a Celtic cross, Paul. What about the glasses?"

"Cool. Did you see the door, too?"

Annmarie squinted her eyes and took a deep breath, "Yes, Paul, I saw it. Again, any luck with those glasses?"

"Nah," Paul answered. "Sorry, A."

Annmarie started to tear up, feeling quite defeated. She sadly decided that it was just one of those once in a lifetime kind of experiences or maybe it had just been another dream—but it had been so different, so real!

They had been searching the cave for quite a while, and the sun was starting to break over the horizon. It wouldn't be long before they would be boarding a plane to fly back home. *Back to the humdrum life of being a nobody*, Annmarie sadly thought to herself. On the other hand, she felt different inside. *Maybe somehow things will be different back home, too.* The sadness lessened as she felt stirrings of hope.

"We should probably head back now," Annmarie sighed.

"Yeah, Sis, let's go," Paul agreed.

Annmarie paused. *He just called me "Sis!"* Her heart melted as she watched him start to walk back home. He turned around and put his flashlight up to his chin, making a crazy face at her. She laughed at his antics.

"You know I'm just your cousin, right?"

"Well, that may be true, but you're still my sister...even though you stink," Paul teased.

Annmarie chased Paul down the hill toward the cottage. When she caught up to him, she gave him a little playful push and proceeded to run ahead of him.

They snuck back into the house and tiptoed into their rooms, stifling their laughter. Annmarie slipped into bed and read her journal entry about her time in the garden so she could remember. Afterwards, she wrote a brand-new entry.

Dear Diary,

I'm so grateful that I was able to come to Ireland!!! Best Trip Ever. Meeting Kennedy and going to the Secret Cave and finding those mystical glasses rocked my world. I will never forget this place as long as I live, and I WILL come back. I'm also really grateful to be with my grandma, grandpa and Paul. It feels good to be with family. Paul called me Sis! I'm so grateful for Kennedy's friendship too. Who knew I could be friends with someone? Maybe I'm friendship material after all. Both Philly and Cardy seem to think so. Still, I'm sad to leave this place. I don't want to go back home to the way things were before. I sure wish I could've found those glasses. I would wear them all the time. I would wear them at school and just be there during classes. No one would know. It would be so awesome! Still...for the first time ever, I think I'm going to be okay.

Annmarie put down her journal and pen and closed her eyes and tried to fall asleep, but she just couldn't. A few moments later, she heard a soft knock on her door.

"Can I come in?" Paul asked softly.

"Sure."

He walked into the room, flopped on her bed and gave her a big hug. A smile erupted on Annmarie's face. Within minutes, they both had fallen asleep.

Chapter 15

A few hours later, they all got up to go to the airport. As they drove, Annmarie glanced over at her grandma and noticed her eyes were glistening. Grandma looked at Annmarie and started to laugh and then cry.

"Grandma, what's wrong? Are you okay?"

At Annmarie's question, everyone's attention turned toward Grandma.

Between sobs she admitted that she didn't want to leave because she was sad they had waited so long to connect with Annmarie and Paul. She said she wanted things to be different going forward.

Grandpa Eli put his arm around Grandma and hugged her. It was as if he caught the emotional bug, and he began crying right along with her.

"I agree. From now on, we are going to be more involved in your lives, okay kids?" Grandpa Eli sniffed, wiping away his tears. Annmarie felt the same, so she started to tear up as well.

Paul responded by laughing at them.

"Don't be silly! You don't have to cry. We are going to be together from now on. Grandpa, we can go fishing on Lake Michigan together this summer. It'll be awesome! Grandma, you and Annmarie can go do girl stuff, too. And you can come to my basketball games!"

After arriving at the airport, the family unloaded their bags, went to their terminal and sat down to wait. Grandma Em surprised everyone with a bag of Lily's heavenly shortbread cookies, and all four eagerly helped themselves.

"I'm going to order these and have Lily send them overseas. I'll pay whatever it takes!" She exclaimed.

"Grandma, how long would it take to ship them to us?" Annmarie asked.

"I don't know, sweetie. I'm guessing it would take a week or so? I would pay extra for speedy shipping though," Grandma Em replied.

As soon as they got onto the plane, Annmarie wondered if she would have another panic attack. Just thinking about it made her heart start to pound out of her chest. She closed her eyes and a picture of Mr. Immanuel's face came into view. As she remembered the love shining from his eyes, that feeling of peace flooded through her body, yet again. She heard his voice say, *"Everything is going to be okay, my ray of sunshine."*

"Hey, A! Grandpa gave me a pack of his cards and said we could play those games he taught us in Ireland. Wanna play with me on the plane?" Paul asked.

Annmarie smiled and nodded her head.

They boarded the plane and found their seats. This time all four of them were sitting in a row instead of being broken up. It felt very indicative of their journey. In the beginning they were separated, but now they were all closer together. Grandma and Grandpa whispered to each other as they looked at Annmarie. She knew they were talking about her, but she pretended not to notice.

As the plane took off, Paul grabbed Annmarie's hand and gave her a squeeze. "Everything is gonna be alright, Sis. I'm here," Paul encouraged.

"I'm good, Paul," Annmarie assured him.

"If you need to lean on someone, lean on me," Paul said.

Paul had suddenly decided he was going to play protective big brother. Annmarie smiled softly at him, thinking it was cute. He was going through a growth spurt, too and soon would be taller than she was.

The flight home was much smoother and less eventful. Annmarie and Paul played cards together for a while and talked about their trip. Paul confided in Annmarie that he would go back one day and marry Kennedy. Rather than scoff, Annmarie simply offered to go with him if he ever did return. And she meant it—she also had her own plan to go back and find those glasses again. The two siblings fell asleep, and when they woke up, the plane was landing.

"I'm so proud of you, Annmarie. You conquered your fear and didn't have any problems flying home," Grandma Em whispered to Annmarie.

Conqueror was a great word! Annmarie never would have used it to describe herself, but that's exactly how she felt. Yet she knew she hadn't done it alone. The peace that came from her time with Mr. Immanuel was what had chased away her anxiety. She hoped she would always remember it so clearly. What if time went on and she forgot his face, or the way he sounded, or the way it had felt to be held in his arms?

Her smile faded as they gathered their belongings and disembarked from the plane. She didn't like the way it felt for her to worry about forgetting, so she gathered up her resolve. *I won't forget! I'll just have to find another way back to the garden, that's all!*

Feeling bolstered by her determination, Annmarie tuned back in to Paul's chatter. She scrunched her nose up at the dragon breath he had developed, but she figured hers probably wasn't much better. She suggested that they take a quick break, brush their teeth and freshen up. Everyone else agreed that was a good idea.

Grandma Em and Annmarie walked into the women's room together.

"Thank you so much for taking me on this trip, Grandma. I've never had so much fun in my life," Annmarie thanked her as she splashed her face with cold water.

After Grandma finished spitting and rinsing out her mouth, she replied, "The pleasure was all ours, Annmarie. We have enjoyed you two so much, and we feel so blessed to have had a 'do-over' with you. I just really hope that Bonnie will open her heart to us as well."

Annmarie nodded in agreement. She understood that their relationship was complicated, and that Bonnie suffered from anger and self-pity. She was unhappy and crabby all the time. Annmarie tried to imagine how Bonnie would react to Grandma and Grandpa wanting more time with them. She hated her parents, so it was an absolute miracle she had allowed them to go on the trip to Ireland in the first place. In fact, Annmarie dreaded going home.

"Any chance I could live with you and Grandpa?" Annmarie asked before she could stop herself. She wanted to take back the question, but it was already floating out there in the atmosphere. She wasn't sure if she wanted to know the answer.

Grandma Em passionately hugged Annmarie.

"It's okay, Grandma. I understand. It wouldn't work anyway, would it? I'm sorry I asked that," Annmarie said.

Grandma Em grabbed her shoulders and very seriously looked her in the eyes.

"Sweet Annmarie. I would love nothing more than to take

you home with me right now, but it is complicated, my dear. I love you so much, but there are some legal hoops that we would need to jump through, and Bonnie has already thrown that in our faces," Grandma Em explained very seriously.

"Okay." Annmarie felt stupid for asking the question, and very uncomfortable. She wiggled out of the grandma hold and swiftly shuffled out the door.

That old, familiar, accusing voice started speaking to her heart, "See, you aren't worth it, Annmarie. You are still unwanted. Some things never change. Welcome back to your miserable reality." Her chest began to constrict, and it took her breath away. The bars of self-loathing surrounded her like an invisible prison. It was physically painful.

"Annmarie, wait!" Grandma Em called after her. "You don't understand!"

Annmarie kept walking toward the gate to get to Paul.

"Please, Annmarie. Wait," Grandma Em pleaded.

Finally, Annmarie turned around to face her because her grandmother's voice had started to rise. Annmarie didn't want her to make an embarrassing scene.

"Bonnie has legal guardianship of you. She has done everything in her power to keep custody. We asked her many years ago to release you to us because you were struggling in school, but Bonnie was not willing to give up custody. We knew if we pressed the issue that she might do something drastic, so we had to back off because she held all the cards."

Confident that she now had Annmarie's attention, Grandma Em sighed and continued, "We also had to weigh the fact that Paul would be lonely without you there. There are so many factors. I would love nothing more than to have a normal, loving relationship with all three of you. Bonnie is hurting, we know that. We have been praying for restoration in our relationship with her for a long time now. Eli and I believe this trip was an answer to prayer. Annmarie, I'm sorry for all you have been through. We love you so much, and we are here for you now." Grandma Em looked at Annmarie with tear-filled eyes, her eyebrows crinkled in an expression pleading with her to understand.

Annmarie soaked in all the words like a sponge. She was wanted? She was blown away that Grandma had wanted to have her many years ago. It was even more complicated than she had understood.

"Wow," Annmarie whispered. "Grandma Em, I'm sorry. I didn't understand. But…I don't want to live with Aunt Bonnie anymore."

"I know, Annmarie, but we are here for you. We love you. This trip has been a gift to me, Annmarie. I'm so glad that we were able to truly connect. I have fresh hope," Grandma said as she hugged her granddaughter. "But, please, don't tell Bonnie that I shared any of this with you. I promised her I wouldn't tell you, and if she knew, I'm afraid she would keep us out of your lives forever!"

"I won't tell, Grandma Em. I promise."

With another hug, the two turned and walked to meet the boys. Annmarie agreed that she also had fresh new hope. So many good, new things had come out of this trip. Still, she walked in a bit of a daze, awestruck at what Grandma Em had told her. They had never rejected her at all! Mr. Immanuel was right: she *was* worthy of love.

After meeting up with Paul and Grandpa Eli, they all journeyed to the baggage claim area. They picked up their luggage and Grandpa Eli insisted on getting the car from the parking lot to pick them up. Grandma, Paul and Annmarie sat down with all the luggage and waited. They were all very happy to have a little respite as they were exhausted from the trip. Paul put his head on Annmarie's shoulder.

Grandpa arrived and loaded the luggage and family into the car. They drove in silence back to Bonnie's apartment. Everyone was tired and hoped that Bonnie would be in a good mood.

"I'm bummed. I don't wanna go home," Paul sulked. Everyone nodded in agreement.

They arrived at the apartment and knocked on the door. No one answered. They knocked again. Still, no answer.

Annmarie fished her key out of her purse to open the door.

"Bonnie? Bonnie are you here?" Grandma Em asked as they entered the small apartment.

No answer.

Paul checked her bedroom and knocked on the bathroom door. The apartment was empty.

"She's probably at work." Paul said.

Grandma Em and Grandpa Eli frowned at each other at the thought that Bonnie wasn't there to greet the kids.

"It's okay, Grandma. It's pretty normal for her to be gone at work," Annmarie assured them.

"I hate to leave you here alone. Eli, do you think we should wait for Bonnie to return?" Grandma asked, worriedly.

"We could stay, Em, if you think it would be best," Grandpa Eli answered.

"It's okay, guys. Paul and I are here alone all the time, and to be honest, we're pretty tired. I know you are, too. You never know how Bonnie will be if she's coming home from work."

33 Annmarie urged them to go. She was really looking forward to having her own quiet time in her room to read her journal again and just sleep.

"Yeah, it's true," Paul agreed. "You guys can go home now. I'm the man of the house."

"Well, if you say so," Grandpa Eli said, beaming with pride. They went in for a big group goodbye hug.

"I'll call you so we can go fishing on Lake Michigan, Grandpa," Paul smiled.

"You betcha, Grandson." Grandpa Eli offered him a high-five.

Grandpa and Grandma finally left, although Grandma Em still wasn't very happy that Bonnie wasn't there to greet them.

Paul and Annmarie sighed deeply and looked knowingly at each other. It was definitely time for a nap. Annmarie hurried to her room, and Paul nestled into the couch. They were both exhausted.

Annmarie flopped on her bed. She was beyond tired, yet was wide awake and unable to fall asleep. She decided to re-read her journal from Ireland. When she read her entry, she felt a physical sensation overtake her that brought her back to the peace she felt in the secret place. She held the precious journal close to her chest. At least this way she knew she wouldn't forget!

Annmarie heard the door open, and she knew that Bonnie had finally come home. Annmarie decided to pretend sleep. She didn't feel like talking with Bonnie, especially after all that Grandma Em had told her. Luckily, Bonnie didn't even check on Annmarie when she came home.

She did hear Bonnie chatting with Paul about the trip though. He excitedly told her about the fishing excursions with Grandpa Eli. Bonnie responded with sarcastic laughter and announced that he shouldn't get used to spending time with them because they were fake and didn't have time for Paul and Annmarie. Paul tried to defend them, but it made Bonnie even more angry, and she started yelling and swearing at him. Annmarie could hear Paul start to cry, which was unusual for him.

Just then Annmarie's bedroom door burst open, and Paul rushed at Annmarie and, like a machine gun, started defending his grandparents again. He wanted to get Annmarie in on the debate. Annmarie rolled over in her bed, uninterested in getting involved in the discussion.

"Annmarie! Grandma and Grandpa said they wanna see us more. They're good people, aren't they?" Paul whined.

Annmarie didn't answer.

Bonnie followed Paul into Annmarie's bedroom. "They are not dependable. They pretend to love you, but then they leave you high and dry. They are not good! I let you go on one trip, and they've already brainwashed you?" Bonnie yelled indignantly. "Well, never again!"

For some reason, Annmarie felt a strength she hadn't known before. She looked at them both and asked a question.

"What's for dinner?" She decided she was not going to play the blame game. She had a newfound love for her grandparents, and she wasn't interested in starting a war with Bonnie over their difference of opinion.

Bonnie and Paul looked at each other bewildered by her question.

"I didn't get to the store, so you're on your own. Make some mac-n-cheese if you're hungry. I'm going to lay down," Bonnie huffed and marched to her bedroom, slamming the door as hard as she could.

"You're wrong about them, Mom!" Paul screamed in a fit of rage and ran out of the apartment.

Although Bonnie didn't budge from her room, Annmarie was worried about Paul, so she got up and ran after him. She spotted him running toward the school and called out for him to stop as she followed.

Finally, he stopped running and fell down on the ground, sobbing. Annmarie lovingly wrapped her arm around him. They sat there for a while as Paul let out his frustration.

"Annmarie," he sniffled as his sobs began to subside. "I never want to go back to that apartment ever again!"

"I know, Paul. It's hard when you don't see eye to eye with someone—especially when it's your mom. She's hurting and having a hard time forgiving Grandma and Grandpa." Annmarie was surprised she was so calm.

Paul looked at Annmarie and wiped his tears on his sleeve.

"I just want to have a normal, happy family. Why is that so hard? Mom didn't see Grandma and Grandpa like we saw. They're not who she says they are. She needs to give them a chance!"

"Paul, everything is going to be okay. Over time you will see. Grandma and Grandpa will not give up on us. They are good, and they are sorry about the past. They're trying to make things right. We can't just tell Bonnie they've changed. She needs to see it with her own eyes to believe it. Give it some time. Paul, I'm here with you on this. Everything will work out."

Paul looked at Annmarie quizzically. "What happened to you?"

"What do you mean?"

"You know. You're like a different person. Something happened to you in Ireland. You *aren't* the same."

Annmarie smiled and shrugged her shoulders. Was it her experience in the garden? She wasn't afraid on the airplane nor was she afraid of Bonnie or the confrontation. She wasn't upset. Normally it would be Paul comforting her, but this was something new.

"I guess I just know down deep that everything will work out," Annmarie tried to explain. "Should we go back home?"

"Okay," Paul said, wiping away more tears.

She gave her little brother one more solid squeeze before helping him to his feet. As they walked home together, her arm around his shoulders, a blanket of warmth surrounded her as she bathed in her newfound wisdom and strength. She couldn't stop thinking of Mr. Immanuel, knowing that he was the source of her transformation.

Chapter 16

School resumed the next day, and as Paul and Annmarie walked to school, Philly made a beeline straight over to say hello. Annmarie looked at her and smiled.

"Hi, Paul. Hi, Annmarie! How was your trip? I can't wait to hear all about it!" Philly asked with an enthusiastic bounce.

"It was great!" Paul said and ran ahead to catch up with some of his friends.

"Annmarie, I love your outfit! Did you get that in Ireland?"

Annmarie blushed, "Oh! Um...yeah, my Grandma bought it for me. You really like it?"

"Of course!" Philly gushed. "That red looks gorgeous on you! And, wow, now I feel like I have to compete with that figure of yours! Who knew you had those curves, girl?! You look like a model in a magazine!"

"Stop it! You're embarrassing me!" Annmarie covered her red cheeks with her hands and changed the subject.

"How was *your* break?" She knew she would get an earful, but at the same time she was actually looking forward to hearing Philly's usual chattiness.

"My break was great! Thanks for asking! We did some sightseeing things around Milwaukee. We went to the zoo, the museum and ate dinner at this fish-fry place where they played live polka music! We took Chewy to this really great dog park, and he made lots of friends. I did miss you though. I'm glad you're back. I bet you got some amazing pictures in Ireland for class. I'm so excited to get our film developed!"

"That sounds great, Philly! The last time I was at the zoo or museum were class field trips in grade school. We should go together sometime."

Philly, amazed and stunned, agreed. Annmarie was just as surprised at the mysterious confidence overcame her. Usually, she was riddled with anxiety when walking into school. She didn't think it was the new clothes. In fact, that would normally make her feel *more* anxious! Paul was right. She was definitely different.

"Philly, I'm glad you had a good time. See you at lunch?"

"I thought you'd never ask!" Philly beamed.

The girls went their separate ways. Annmarie walked to class with a spring in her step. She knew she would pass Janice on the way, but she decided just to ignore her.

"Hey, Annmarie! Heard you went to Ireland. Did you kiss any leprechauns?" Janice taunted. She laughed and so did other kids around her.

Annmarie smirked, shook her head, and just let it roll off her back. It felt good to let it go and simply get to class. A smile even spread across her face.

When lunch rolled around, she connected with Philly. No one else wanted to sit with them, and they were totally fine with that. They chatted about their break, but it was mostly Annmarie listening to Philly tell stories about her dog Chewy. She didn't mind. She did, however, share a little about the beauty of Ireland and how Paul was obsessed with catching the Loch Ness Monster.

Philly cocked her head to the side and squinted inquisitively at her friend. "Annmarie, there's something different about you. You seem more relaxed or something. What happened to you?"

"I don't know," Annmarie shrugged. She hadn't said much. She wondered if she somehow looked different on the outside. "Why? Am I glowing neon or something?"

Philly giggled and shook her head.

As Philly launched into another thread of excitement regarding her vacation, Annmarie caught a glimpse of Jonathan in the corner of her eye. Standing at the other end of the lunchroom, he was staring directly at her. As soon as their eyes met, he nodded and smiled exactly the same way he had in Mr. Immanuel's garden. He then grabbed his tray and walked to his usual lunch table.

Annmarie's heart raced. *Did that just happen?* She wanted so badly to ask him about her experience in Ireland, but how could she? What if it was all just a big glorified dream? She would look so stupid.

That familiar condemning voice piped up in her ear, warning her that she would be a fool to ask. Oh, but the desire to talk to him burned in her heart like a wildfire. She hoped for a chance meeting.

"Annmarie? What the heck was that? Is there something going on with Jonathan that I need to know about?" Philly prodded.

Jerked out of her thoughts, Annmarie stuttered, "I...Um...No?"

"Annmarie! What is going on?" Philly asked before she could even get her words out. "Come out with it!"

"Philly, I don't know what's going on. He was probably looking at someone else nearby." Annmarie looked around her to see if any of his friends were around but there was no one else. All of his friends were already sitting at his table.

"Um, yeah. Okay," Philly's voice dripped with disbelief. "That was weird. That was not a casual glance, Annmarie!"

"Do I have lettuce in my teeth or a big zit somewhere on my face?" Annmarie asked Philly, suddenly convinced that he must've seen something wrong with her. She proceeded to touch her face and teeth to make sure.

"Wow," Philly laughed sarcastically. "No, Annmarie. He was clearly staring straight at you and then smiled like he had a secret."

Annmarie excused herself and ran to the bathroom to get out of the firing line of questions.

What is going on with me? She thought to herself. *Get it together, Annmarie. That was not normal. Gosh, his face is so dreamy. Am I nuts?* Annmarie splashed some water on her face and dried it off with a scratchy brown paper towel.

She looked into the mirror and with determination spoke aloud to her reflection, "You are going to talk to Jonathan Walters about this." As she turned to exit the bathroom, she inadvertently heard two girls talking, and one said very loudly to the other, "You should totally do that!"

To Annmarie, it was as though this girl was cheering her on. She knew the words weren't given with the intention of her hearing them, but they were like a heavenly confirmation that she should just do it!

The last hour of school finally came, and Annmarie was excited to bring in and develop her film from Ireland. Mrs. Smith announced that they would be taking turns in the lab to develop their pictures from spring break. They were to select three of their top pictures to be developed into an 8x10 for display in the library. Along with the pictures, each student was to write a paragraph explaining their significance.

142

"Annmarie, aren't you excited to see the pictures you took in Ireland? I have some pretty cool pictures, I think. Chewy and I went for walks and to some local parks and we found some cool…"

Philly's voice trailed off and faded into the background as Annmarie fell into a daydream about Mr. Immanuel's hug and the loving feeling it had brought her.

"Hello? Annmarie? Anyone there?" Philly reached out and shook Annmarie's arm.

"Oh! Yes. Sorry, Philly…What?" Annmarie sheepishly refocused on her friend.

"I was asking you about what your favorite picture might be from the trip. You zoned out."

"Oh, well, I met a girl named Kennedy in Ireland. She took me to the top of this big hill. I'm guessing I'll like the pictures I took there the best."

"That sounds so cool," Philly said with a smile. "Hey, Annmarie, I know you aren't really allowed to have visitors and stuff after school, but I was wondering if you'd want to come hang out at my house sometime after school if we plan it? My mom makes a really good shortbread cookie that's like eating a slice of heaven."

Annmarie smiled, thinking of Lily's scrumptious shortbreads. Hard to believe anyone could make shortbreads that good. Almost instinctively, she blurted, "Sure. I'll ask my aunt."

Annmarie was even more surprised at her ready acceptance to the invitation than Philly. Recovering quickly, Philly gasped excitedly, "Great! Let me know what day works for you, and I'll put in the order."

Although she was still a bit surprised at her quick acceptance of Philly's invitation, she smiled. "The lady who took care of our house in Ireland made us shortbread cookies that I still dream about. They melted in my mouth! So, I have a new-found love for shortbreads. You made just the right offer!"

Philly was speechless. She was flabbergasted to hear Annmarie speak more than a few words at once! Annmarie was completely different, but if this was the result, she wasn't going to jinx it by asking anymore questions.

After school, Paul had basketball practice, so Annmarie packed up her belongings and started happily walking home. What a breakthrough day! She had let her guard down with Philly, Janice's snarky comment had rolled off her back, and the cherry on top was locking eyes with Jonathan in the lunchroom. His sparkling smile left her weak in the knees!

That night, Annmarie decided to make spaghetti and garlic bread for dinner. She decided to go above and beyond and bake a cake, too. She was in such a good mood, she was oozing excitement.

As she went through the refrigerator, she noticed they were out of parmesan cheese, so she decided to see if Ms. Opal had some to borrow.

Annmarie knocked on Ms. Opal's door, and almost mid-knock, Ms. Opal answered with a great big mama-bear hug.

"Oh, my sweet little Annmarie! How are you sweetheart? Oh, how I missed seeing you around here. How was your trip? Come in, come in!" Ms. Opal pulled out a kitchen chair for Annmarie. "I made some chocolate chip cookies for you and Paul." Ms. Opal filled a plate and slid it before Annmarie.

Annmarie thanked Ms. Opal and ate a cookie. She shared with Ms. Opal little pieces about the trip. She told her how Paul was determined to find the Loch Ness Monster with Grandpa. Ms. Opal had a booming laugh that shook the walls of her apartment. Her laughter was extremely contagious, and Annmarie couldn't help but join in.

Annmarie shared about connecting with Grandma and Grandpa, the delicious food, and even their new friends, Lily and Kennedy. She divulged Paul's monster crush on her and Kennedy's nickname, Cardy. Still, Annmarie held back

144

telling her about the secret place. It was just too out there—too profound to share.

Ms. Opal gave Annmarie a contemplative gaze.

"There's something different about you, little lady. I can't put my finger on it, but it's like you've grown or matured since you've been gone. Did you grow?" Ms. Opal put her hands on her hips. "Yes, you must have grown."

Annmarie wasn't really sure how to respond. "Um, well, Ms. Opal, thank you for the cookies. It was so nice to see you. I missed you, too. Anyway, I was going to make some spaghetti. I wanted to surprise Bonnie and Paul, and I was wondering if you had any parmesan cheese that I could borrow—and I wanted to invite you over for dinner too!"

Annmarie couldn't believe she had asked Ms. Opal over for dinner and suddenly got extremely nervous. Aunt Bonnie might not approve of her asking without permission. Ms. Opal could tell Annmarie was nervous, and she knew Bonnie.

"Oh, sweet girl, aren't you precious? Yes, of course I have parmesan for you, but I will take a rain check on dinner. I have my ladies' group tonight." With a smile, Ms. Opal handed Annmarie the parmesan and a plate of cookies.

"Thank you, Ms. Opal."

"You bet." Ms. Opal gave Annmarie another mama-bear hug and escorted her across the hall to her own apartment.

Annmarie started making the spaghetti right away. By the time Aunt Bonnie came home, it was ready and on the table. She was home a little early.

When Bonnie walked into the apartment, she crinkled her nose in confusion and asked, "Annmarie, what are you doing?"

"Hi, Aunt Bonnie!" Annmarie greeted her with an excited smile. "I had a great idea and thought I would make you and Paul a nice spaghetti dinner and dessert. I know you work hard, so I thought you'd enjoy a nice meal."

Bonnie, eyes wide like a deer caught in the headlights, seemed unsure of how to respond. "Um, why the sudden urge to do something nice?"

"I just wanted to," Annmarie shrugged. "I even added extra garlic and Italian spices to the sauce. When we were in Ireland, Grandma shared some cooking secrets with me." As soon as the words were out of her mouth, she realized that she shouldn't have mentioned it. Bonnie scowled as soon as she mentioned Grandma's name.

Bonnie brusquely turned away, "Well, I have a headache." She grabbed a small plastic bowl out of the cupboard and poured herself some cereal instead. She often ate cereal when she wasn't feeling well because she said the milk helped calm her stomach. As she marched herself and her cereal to her bedroom, she snapped, "Make sure you clean up this ugly mess when you're done."

Annmarie was disappointed but not surprised. She put Bonnie's place setting back in the cupboard, but she knew Paul would enjoy her spaghetti. Paul loved food. Lots of food.

Sure enough, he bounded into the apartment about thirty minutes later, enthusiastic about the surprise meal.

"Hey, A! Wow! Spaghetti? Cake? Cookies? What's the occasion? This is awesome!" Paul was all smiles.

Annmarie grinned at his eagerness, but warned, "Shhh, Paul! Aunt Bonnie has a headache, so keep the volume down!"

"Oops, sorry!" Paul respectfully lowered his volume, but his face was still beaming. "This is sweet! Thanks! I'm starving!" Paul dove right into the saucy spaghetti goodness.

The two chatted about their day and how it had been a good one for both of them. Paul was even excited for Annmarie to get her pictures of Ireland developed. Especially the ones of him holding his big catch! Annmarie noticed he had made Kennedy's picture his screensaver on his phone. She laughed, but he simply reiterated that he was going to Ireland to marry her one day.

"Basketball practice was a beast today! Even walking home was hard—my legs feel like jello! I was super happy when J-Walz picked me up and gave me a ride home!"

Annmarie tried to play it cool, but just hearing Jonathan's name made her blush. It was just too hard to cover up her reaction.

Knowing he had pushed a button, Paul started to laugh.

Although Annmarie normally would have been mortified and gotten angry, this time after a brief hesitation, she just began laughing right along with him.

"Quiet out there!" Aunt Bonnie screamed from her room.

"Shhhh!" Annmarie whispered loudly, trying to stifle her giggles.

"Sorry, Mom!" Paul shouted back, with a smirk.

Annmarie rolled her eyes and shook her head. "Quiet, or you'll get us both killed!"

Paul began laughing again, and spaghetti spurted from Paul's mouth onto the table, which began a new terrible chorus of snorting and muffled laughing. They laughed until they both started crying. Annmarie was seriously afraid that Bonnie would come out and knock their heads together. But something inside both of them had snapped, and they couldn't control the laughter.

"If I have to come out there…" Bonnie warned in a louder tone than before.

They both knew that if they were going to save their lives, they would either have to stop laughing or get out of the apartment. It was raining outside so they opted to separate and try to relax. Annmarie ran to her room, still full of giggles. Paul flopped on the couch and covered his head with a pillow.

Finally, Annmarie caught her breath and noticed she was smiling. She didn't feel alone at all, and a weight had lifted off of her. She felt refreshed and rejuvenated after their laughter fit. She texted Paul goodnight with the sleepy face emoji. Paul texted back that he would clean up the kitchen. Annmarie was grateful. Really grateful.

Chapter 17

As the week went on and Annmarie got her chance in the photo lab, she remembered the last time she had been there with Jonathan and how kind he had been to help her. She went through the steps of developing her negatives and then took a loop to examine them.

She had to select three to blow up for the display. She had a really funny picture of Paul staring in wonder at Kennedy and another of him with his big catch. There were quite a few of the picnic and the hillside vista that were possibilities as well.

She looked really closely at the cave pictures, and one negative took her breath away. She noticed what looked like the mystical glasses in the lower left corner of the shot. She gasped with amazement. Her heart pounding, she looked into the loop once again and clear as day, there they were!

Since she had returned from Ireland, she had tried to convince herself that it all must have been a silly dream. The whole thing made no sense. However, here she saw with her own eyes the truth. She really had found the glasses and she really had gone into a different realm. Maybe it was a dream world?

She went right to work getting the negatives ready to be transposed onto the photo paper. She could hardly wait to see it up close. *What a gift*, she thought to herself. *This is the most exciting life-changing picture of all time!* Overwhelmed and shaking in the face of the evidence, she felt a newfound boldness to find Jonathan and ask him about the secret place.

After school, Annmarie connected with Philly as they had planned to hang out at her house that day. Annmarie had miraculously gotten permission from Bonnie to go.

Annmarie grabbed Philly and said urgently, "Philly, I have to talk to Jonathan right away! Can I meet you at your house in a little while?"

"Annmarie, you're scaring me a little. What is going on? Can I help?"

"No Philly. Please believe me, I just have to ask him something. I'll be over as soon as I can!" Annmarie was overwhelmed with the need to talk to Jonathan and verify once and for all if her experience had been real or only concocted in her own mind.

"Okay. No problem—but you'd better fill me in when you come over!" Philly insisted.

"Okay," Annmarie nodded absently, swiveling her head to see if she could catch a glimpse of her target.

"Oh, I just saw him going down toward the gym. Maybe he has practice. You'd better hurry," Philly suggested.

Annmarie ran toward the gym and saw Jonathan talking with some other guys. He was so perfect! She was breaking all of her own rules of engagement by approaching him, but she boldly walked up and tapped him on the shoulder. He turned around and smiled down at her.

"What's up?" He asked.

"I…I…Um." Annmarie froze as his friends, all popular basketball players, stared quizzically at her. She was suddenly intensely intimidated.

Jonathan looked at her without breaking his smile even at her awkwardness. "Hey, I'm glad you stopped over. I needed to ask you something. Hey, guys I'll be right back," He shot over his shoulder at his friends, as he led her to a more private area where they could talk.

"Thanks," Annmarie said with a relieved sigh. He was her knight in shining armor.

"Hey, what's good?" Jonathan asked still smiling. Annmarie swore she saw a twinkle in his eye. She was mesmerized by his face.

"Well, um. This might sound strange…" Annmarie shakily said.

Jonathan put his hand on Annmarie's shoulder. "Don't be nervous, Annmarie. It's okay."

His hand carried the same weight and atmosphere of peace that she had felt in the secret place. She was already getting goosebumps.

"I don't know how to say this, but I saw you when I was in Ireland. I mean, I was in some kind of weird dream or something. There were these glasses and when I put them on—I just know I saw you there, and I know you saw me too. Does this make sense to you, or am I crazy?"

Jonathan smiled at her, and suddenly he spoke to her, clear as crystal inside of her head! Although his lips never moved, he said, "You're not crazy."

Annmarie gasped and took a shocked step backward.

Jonathan chuckled. "Yes, Annmarie. We saw each other but we weren't in Ireland."

Annmarie was blown away, hanging on every word.

"I found these glasses in a cave in Ireland and when I put them on, I was in this beautiful, peaceful place. I don't know

how to describe it other than, like, the Wizard of Oz."
Annmarie felt a little less nervous and more curious, instead.

"Cardy led you there."

"Yes! How do you know Kennedy?" Annmarie asked.

Jonathan just chuckled. "I have practice here soon. Can you meet me after practice to talk more?"

"Yes. When?" Annmarie eagerly asked.

"In a few hours. Where can I meet you?"

Annmarie was dumbfounded and just stared at him blankly.

"I've got an idea. Why don't we meet at Fischer Park at the bench by the playground? What's your phone number? I'll text you when I leave practice." Jonathan kept looking back at the gym where his friends were waiting for him.

"Sure!" Annmarie gave him her number. Was this really happening? He gave Annmarie a head nod and jogged over to the gym locker room to get ready for practice.

Annmarie couldn't put her finger on all the emotions she carried. She didn't know whether to cry or laugh or faint. Jogging all the way to Philly's house, she replayed the conversation with Jonathan over and over. She felt like little orphan Annie who struck it rich with Daddy Warbucks.

This was all too extravagant for her to wrap her mind around. *I hope he has an extra pair of glasses!* She fantasized about revisiting sweet Mr. Immanuel and even went so far as to imagine her and Jonathan exchanging wedding vows there one day—*Hold the phone, you're getting carried away!*

She wondered how her little garden was doing, too. There were still so many questions about this whole mystery. She couldn't wait to meet Jonathan again and get some answers. It was scandalous that the most popular guy in school would take time to connect with her, the nobody. She erupted into a full-blown belly laugh as she reached for the doorbell at Philly's house.

Philly answered the door and was stunned. She had never witnessed Annmarie laugh like this.

"What is so funny? Why are we laughing?" Philly asked as Chewy charged, barking and jumping up on Annmarie's legs. "Chewy, down boy. Sorry, Annmarie, he always does this with guests."

Annmarie bent down to get face to face with Chewy. "Hi Chewy. Aww, aren't you cute!" He wagged his tail fiercely as he licked her face. Annmarie laughed even harder as Chewy's tongue went up her nostril.

Before they knew it, Philly and Annmarie fell into a laughing fit complete with snorting. Finally, Philly caught her breath and asked if there was food in her teeth as she grinned as big as she could. That triggered yet another fit of laughter that took a few minutes to pass.

"Something smells delicious, Philly."

"Come on in the kitchen. Mom's cookies are still warm. She's outside in the backyard getting her flower beds ready. Come outside and I'll introduce you before we have cookies." Philly led Annmarie to the backyard.

Annmarie giggled again even at the word flower bed thinking of the garden. What are the odds. There were so many parallels to Ireland with the cookies, the garden and the crazy dog licking.

"Hey, Mom. This is Annmarie. Annmarie, meet my mom." Philly said.

Philly's mom looked up and smiled and waved at the girls. "Hi, Annmarie. Happy to meet you. Philly has told me lots of good things about you," she said, wiping the sweat from her forehead.

Annmarie smiled and wondered what exactly Philly had told her. Annmarie hadn't exactly been warm and friendly with her. "Nice to meet you, too." she replied.

Philly was already pushing Annmarie back into the kitchen toward the table and the plate of cookies. She poured some milk and brought the glasses over. Chewy sat expectantly looking up at Annmarie, hoping for scraps.

"Alright, lady. What is up with you? Did you find Jonathan? What did he say? Oh, my goodness, don't keep me in the dark. What in the world happened?"

"I really don't have much to share right now. Yes, I did see Jonathan, and we are going to talk after practice. It's a long story."

"Honestly Annmarie, you'd better fill me in when you can. I know something is up. But man, you have changed since you've been back from Ireland. I have to tell you; I saw a lot of potential in you from the first day we met. I just knew it wouldn't be long, and we would be really good friends." Philly said emphatically.

"People keep telling me that I'm different. I do feel different. I feel happier." Annmarie stumbled with the words to explain her feelings.

"I have this philosophy—a 'Philly-osophy'—that when I see someone who is shy or insecure, it means they've been knocked around because there's something really special inside of them. Why else would they try to knock you down? It's a jealousy thing." Philly explained.

Annmarie looked at her quizzically. "I'm pretty sure nobody is jealous of me. I'm pretty much a nobody."

Philly chuckled to herself. "You are really special, Annmarie. Every single person has a gift inside. Some people try to block others' gifts so their's seem more special. Sometimes you just need someone else to help you see it for yourself."

Annmarie was really not sure how to respond. She sounded very wise, reminding her a bit of Mr. Immanuel.

"Ever since you've come back from Ireland, I just see you opening up more, kind of like a flower blooming. I know that sounds really sappy and weird, but you're coming out of your cave."

Annmarie examined Philly in amazement. "Did I tell you about the cave in Ireland?!"

"Oh yeah, that's right. You did tell me about a cave on a hill or something. That's funny. I wasn't even thinking of that. Tell me more about your trip, Annmarie," Philly urged.

Annmarie understood now why Philly pursued her in friendship the way she had. She had seen "potential" in her. Philly had seen something no one else had.

"I've never shared this with anyone before, but I have always seen myself hiding like a turtle in a shell," Annmarie shared. Surprisingly, she felt her eyes become misty.

Annmarie opened up about her fear of flying. She shared about feeling insecure and how she met the beautiful Kennedy who surprised her with her kindness. She told Philly about her grandparents and how they completely astounded her in how different they were from what she had been led to believe by her aunt. She shared how much fun they had together and how Grandpa had taken Paul fishing every day while they were there. She described the hill and the cave but stopped just shy of the mystical side of her journey. She wasn't ready to go there yet, but she opened up more to Philly than she ever had with anyone else in a very long time.

"Wow, Annmarie. It looks like you're on a road to a brand-new beginning. You know what? You are brave to share all this with me, and you are so very brave to go that far away with people you barely know," Philly said. "I know how intimidating it can be to go somewhere far from what you're familiar with. But every time I've had to make a move, I remind myself that the struggle has made me bolder and stronger."

"Me? Brave? You know, before the trip, I would have laughed in your face if you called me brave. But now, well…maybe I'm beginning to see it."

Annmarie had never thought of herself as being brave but nodded her head in agreement as she realized bravery must be part of the Annmarie she truly was. It had definitely taken courage to walk right up to Jonathan at school. Yes. She was feeling more confident than ever before, and it felt really good.

"Yep. I see it all over you. Brave is what you are! Hey, do you still remember the card game your grandpa taught you? I have some cards in this drawer over here. Wanna teach me?"

"Yeah, sure." Annmarie said. "But I have to meet Jonathan in a little while. He's going to text me, and then I'll have to get going."

Philly gave her a thumbs up and fetched the cards out of the drawer. They played cards and ate more cookies until finally Annmarie got a text from Jonathan.

"Hey, Philly. I have to get going. Thank you for the cookies and the talk. I really like your 'Philly-osophy.'"

Philly confidently gave Annmarie a warm hug.

"I sure hope you tell me what's going on soon with Jonathan. Do you like him? Does he like you?" Philly exploded.

Annmarie giggled. "I don't think he'd ever like me like that."

"Hmmmmm. I don't know, Annmarie. I think he likes you." Philly said.

Annmarie blushed. "Yeah, right." Yet, her heart began to race in excitement. *Maybe?*

"Okay, well, let me know what happens!" Philly demanded.

Annmarie scooted out the front door and headed toward the park, shaking all the way. She knew this conversation could be a life-changer. Could Philly actually be right? Could he maybe even like her? It seemed to be quite impossible. She encouraged herself to be brave no matter what.

Before she knew it, she was at Fischer Park and found the bench and sat down. He wasn't there yet, so she nervously played a game on her phone and waited.

A moment later, she felt a tap on the shoulder and looked up fully expecting to see Jonathan's face, but it was Janice, her friend Julia, and a few other girls.

"Hey, loser. What are you doing here?" Janice snickered.

Annmarie did her best to ignore the taunting. She clammed up, not wanting to engage with them, bracing herself for the worst.

"Hey, we're talking to you, weirdo," Julia sneered.

Again, Annmarie stared into her phone as if they weren't there. She wasn't sure what to do, but all that bravery she had felt moments earlier evaporated into thin air.

"Annmarie, what's your problem? Did you forget how to talk?" Janice asked getting in her face.

From a short distance, Jonathan saw what was going on and quietly snuck up behind the girls, startling them as they were interrogating Annmarie.

"Hey, what's up?" He asked.

The girls all turned to see him peering over their shoulders. "Oh, Hey J-Walz. How's it going?" Julia asked with a nervous laugh.

"I'm chill." He said as he made his way through the girls to sit next to Annmarie on the bench. Janice, Julia and the others watched in amazement as he put his arm around her.

"Sooo, what is going on here?" Janice hissed.

"I'm here to hang out with Annmarie," Jonathan answered coolly.

"What? Really? But she doesn't talk. Haven't you noticed that?" Julia asked in disbelief.

"Sure, she does." Jonathan shook his head at them and turned to Annmarie. "Are you ready to get going, Annmarie?"

Annmarie nodded.

The girls were stunned speechless. The school's hottest guy with the school's biggest loser? They stood frozen in disbelief as they watched Jonathan escort Annmarie to his car and politely open the door for her.

Annmarie looked down, completely embarrassed by the confrontation. Janice had a way of making her feel powerless and stupid.

"Annmarie. They don't know you. It's time to erase what they say or think." Jonathan assured her. "By the way, Janice isn't your problem."

Annmarie picked up her head and turned to tell Jonathan what a loser she really was, but when their eyes met all she could see was kindness as brilliant as the sun staring back at her. It was as though beams of a truth-laser were shooting from his eyes, supernaturally breaking off the bits of shrapnel stuck in her skin from the exchange with her bullies.

She felt woozy and a bit weak—exactly like she had felt when Mr. Immanuel embraced her in the garden. Tears flooded her eyes and the dam that held them ruptured and she gave in to sobs. Jonathan put his arm around her to comfort her.

"It's okay, Annmarie. Just let it out," He instructed. "Let it *all* out."

Finally, when she was able to gather herself together, she felt a rush of cleansing—a refreshing, cool shower washing away the pain and failure.

"Thank you," Annmarie whispered.

"So, you wanted to know about the garden, right?" Jonathan asked changing the subject.

"Yes!"

"Annmarie, this place is more real than you think. We call it The Good Land. The glasses were just a vehicle to help you see it. Once you've been there, you are a welcomed guest for the rest of your life—all you have to do is close your eyes, see it, and you are there."

"What? I don't get it." Annmarie said. "How do I close

my eyes and then see it? How does that work?"

"Annmarie, The Good Land is inside you. To be honest, Mr. Immanuel wants everyone to find him in The Good Land. He told me how much he loves you and wanted you to visit." Jonathan laughed, "He is actually quite creative. His plan was to get you to the glasses in the cave. He's the one who gave you the dreams about going there, but he knew you would need some kind of physical way to get you in. The vacation, the dreams, meeting Kennedy, seeing me in the garden: it was all a setup orchestrated by Mr. Immanuel himself. Just for you."

Annmarie sat quietly for a moment, trying to process all of this new information. Like a slideshow, she replayed all of the signs she had thought were coincidence that were actually Mr. Immanuel's plan to get her to The Good Land.

She remembered her dreams of the cave, the voice telling her to walk through the door, the doorway carving, which matched the physical cave perfectly. She remembered following Ruby in her dream and seeing cardinals everywhere: outside, in Mrs. Opal's apartment, on her journal in the airport, and even where one should never have been—outside her room in Ireland. Even her new friend, Cardy, was the one who led her to the real cave. His plan was so intricate!

"Mr. Immanuel loves me that much? How does he even know me?"

"He has known you all your life. He created you! He thinks you are beautiful and special." He paused and then continued, "And from what I can see, I think you're pretty special, too." The normally unruffled boy's cheeks flooded with color.

Annmarie was speechless. She couldn't fathom it: the one who created her composed this elaborate plan to get her to The Good Land because he loved her? For a moment, she started to wonder if Jonathan was pulling her leg, but he just knew too much for it to be a joke.

Jonathan cleared his throat to cover up his embarrassment. "Listen, Annmarie. Tonight, before you fall asleep, close your eyes and ask Mr. Immanuel to help you see The Good Land. Wait a little while and you *will* begin to see it. You need to see it in your heart. Don't give up too quickly—be patient. You are welcome to come and go there as you please."

Sensing that Annmarie was still very uncertain about the prospect that she could return to The Good Land anytime she wanted, he continued, "I'm usually up pretty late, so if you are having trouble, feel free to call me."

Jonathan looked down at his watch. "Come on, let me drive you home."

After a few minutes of driving, Annmarie couldn't hold it in any longer. "Jonathan, this is all crazy!"

"Yep. It's pretty sweet," Jonathan said as he drove.

She shook her head with exasperation. "That's not exactly what I meant, Jonathan."

He chuckled but didn't answer.

Jonathan dropped her off at the apartment and flashed her his sparkling smile as he waved goodbye. She watched him drive off and out of sight, and she pinched herself. Walking into the apartment building, she understood what people meant when they said they were walking on air. She was floating on cloud nine. She reached the top of her stairs and ran into Ms. Opal who greeted her with a bear hug.

"Well, if it isn't my sweet Annmarie! How are you, sweet thing?" Ms. Opal asked.

"Hi, Ms. Opal. I'm good. How are you?"

"Oh, honey. I'm doing just fine. I'm getting ready to go to my group. You look a little dreamy right now. I know that look. It's a boy, isn't it?"

Annmarie felt her whole face flush into a nice shade of scarlet, but she laughed and said, "Maybe."

"Oh, my sweet girl is getting all grown up! We should

chat later. I want to hear all about it. I have to get going now, but you be sure to stop and visit soon. I made some more of my famous banana bread," Ms. Opal offered as she scooted out the door.

"Okay, Ms. Opal. I will!"

Ms. Opal stopped at the stairwell, turned around slowly and said, "Why, Annmarie, I do believe you are smiling. You just lit up this whole apartment complex with that glorious smile." With that, she blew Annmarie a kiss and set off.

That night went by with a blur. She was in the apartment with Bonnie and Paul and couldn't help smiling all night long. She couldn't even wait to go to bed to see if she could somehow get to The Good Land again.

"What are you so happy about, Annmarie?" Bonnie asked sarcastically.

Annmarie shrugged her shoulders. She knew Bonnie wouldn't understand her secret. Joy was exploding like an atomic bomb on the inside, and everyone was noticing. She wasn't even trying to; she just was filled with a hope she hadn't ever experienced before.

Her joy was even contagious: Paul was feeling it and smiling along with Annmarie. It had become substantial and seemed to take over the room. Bonnie couldn't understand it, but even she seemed to lighten up a bit in the presence of Annmarie's joy.

Finally, Annmarie retired to her bedroom and nervously laid on her bed, doing exactly as Jonathan had suggested. She closed her eyes, and although she felt foolish, she whispered, "Mr. Immanuel, please help me to come visit you again."

A few minutes passed. Nothing. Five more minutes passed. Nothing. Ten more minutes passed. Nothing. She was getting a little discouraged. Just as she was ready to give up and let it go, she saw Mr. Immanuel and the garden in the background deep in her heart. He was there!

161

She wanted to be closer to him, and in response to her desire she was with him again, feeling the warmth of the sun on her face, the cool breeze brushing her skin as it carried the fragrant aroma of flowers.

"Welcome back, Annmarie." Beams of love-light shot out Mr. Immanuel's eyes, fully embracing her like a blanket of peace. Annmarie threw herself into his arms, and he held her firmly to his chest. She was undone with joy, elated to be near him again.

She looked up and saw Jonathan standing next to them. He was here, too! Instantly, the three of them were transported to the patch that Mr. Immanuel and Annmarie had planted together. The jeweled seeds had blossomed into happy sunflowers and daisies.

They were more than alive! They were vibrant and breathtaking, and it seemed like they were singing a joyful song and waving at her in the refreshing breeze. The soil was dark and moist and the grass around the perimeter was emerald green. Where death had tried to choke this sweet garden, life had now taken over. Annmarie was so happy to see the transformation in her garden and instantly she realized that this unique garden represented what had happened inside of herself!

A powerful hope filled her heart. She knew everything in her life would be okay.

She caught a glimpse of curly red hair and saw Kennedy talking to an older woman over a collection of orchids. Kennedy looked up to meet her gaze. With a grin, she excitedly gestured to the woman and pointed at Annmarie. As she turned, Annmarie recognized Mrs. Opal!

Hearing the sound of her name, Annmarie turned to see Philly jumping and waving both arms in the air, as though she needed rescue. However, the huge grin on her face instead told a story of love and excitement as she began running to greet Annmarie.

She felt Jonathan's hand take hold of hers. "Come on, Annmarie! There's so much we have to show you!"

As she and Jonathan ran to join her friends, Annmarie knew she was loved. This truth was the greatest revelation of her life, but she still didn't quite realize it. There was so much more to discover.

"You are loved, Annmarie." She heard Mr. Immanuel's voice, and it penetrated directly into her heart.

I am loved, Annmarie agreed.

About the Author

Kristen Adam is a community relations specialist living in the Good Land of Wauwatosa, Wisconsin. She enjoys singing, texting and watching musical theater with her husband and two teenage daughters. Kristen is a speaker and avid journal writer. Kristen crafts a devotional piece in a bi-monthly newsletter for an organization very dear to her heart—Soles For Jesus. She is also the proud President of the Wauwatosa West Theater Booster Club. She holds a degree in Communications and Public Relations, and her heart is for every person to know how uniquely loved they are.